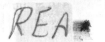

DO NOT REMOVE
CARDS FROM POCKET

TROUBLE BRAND

A year-long manhunt ends in the North Texas cowtown of Lariat when Ranger Dick Rufus gets his man—and finds himself embroiled in a whole mess of trouble. Sided by Jim Harper and oldster 'Lobo' Grant, Dick becomes the target for hired guns, a crooked lawman and banker, a rich rancher and a ruthless woman. The bone of contention is a small ranch, nicknamed 'Trouble Brand', which Dick takes over and defends when the owner is outlawed. Amidst bloody gun-battles, mystery and intrigue, Dick finds a solution.

TROUBLE BRAND

Russ Kidd

A Lythway Book

CHIVERS PRESS
BATH

First published in Great Britain 1984
by
Robert Hale Limited
This Large Print edition published by
Chivers Press
by arrangement with
Robert Hale Limited
1988

ISBN 0 7451 0685 4

British Library Cataloguing in Publication Data

Kidd, Russ
    Trouble Brand.—(A Lythway book).
    Rn: Cyril Donson   I. Title
    823'.914[F]   PR6054.O5

    ISBN 0–7451–0685–4

Photoset, printed and bound in Great Britain by
REDWOOD BURN LIMITED, Trowbridge, Wiltshire

For
my good friend
Lloyd Forster

TROUBLE BRAND

CHAPTER ONE

Dick Rufus finished the last dregs of Java from the tin mug, and drew pleasurably on the cheroot between strong white teeth. He stared at the dying embers of his fire, at peace with the world and in no great rush to get moving.

His camp, well-sheltered between the two towering peaks of the last two southerly prominences of the Rockies, had afforded him a good night's sleep. The mountain tops were already haloed in gold in the east and the shadows of night began to retreat. He was a tall, muscular, yet lean man, broad of shoulder. There were laughter lines around the strong mouth, a suggestion in the blue eyes that he was always about to burst into laughter. But the set of square jaw suggested another side to his nature.

He wore a single Colt's .44 in his gun-belt holster, a fast-draw cut-away rig that might have told a man plenty, and maybe advised cautious treatment of this young man, even when he was laughing.

Two fifteen-hand horses were grazing, loosely tethered, on sparse grass in this mountain valley. One was a roan-bay with spots of grey and white, the other a black stallion. Both were good animals built for stamina and, when the

1

occasion might call for it, a powerful turn of speed.

Dick reflected on his trials and tribulations of the past twelve months since he'd quit the Texas Rangers for personal reasons. Starting out from San Antonio he'd travelled 450 miles to Fort Sumner in New Mexico. There he'd lost the trail. He'd gone on to Sante Fe where luck set him back on the trail. A man he'd talked to had seen a knife fight in a saloon there between a big feller with a vee-shaped scar just below his neck hollow, and a woodsman who was part-Indian.

So he'd taken to the old 1845 Sante Fe trail riding another hundred miles to Las Vegas. A false lead at Fort Sumner had caused him to waste some days hunting around the country near Stinking Springs, where, six years ago in 1881, Pat Garrett had shot Billy the Kid.

Further information gleaned in Las Vegas had sent him off the Santa Fe trail which, from Vegas, wound north to Wagon Mound, then north-east to Raton and on to Bent's Fort. He'd headed almost due east through the mountains planning to come out about fifty miles north of Amarillo. The country below this had been torn by the Texas Range War for ten years until less than a year ago. Once he struck the open country his trail would take him north almost to the border of Oklahoma where the big landrush of 1849 had spilled over into Texas.

He'd heard vaguely of the new frontier town

2

Lariat but his duties had never taken him there.

The big red sun was climbing above the mountain tops when he doused his fire and collected his possibles, packing them neatly in a roll tied to the big stallion.

He threw his saddle onto the roan, secured it, checked the load in his Winchester seventeen-shot, and slid the weapon into the long saddle holster.

He climbed aboard and kneed the roan forward into a steady canter, trailing the black behind on a leadrope ... 'Today,' he announced to the mountains and the trees, 'is my birthday, August 6th, 1887. Maybe, this day of my one quarter century, something good will happen, huh?'

Before very long he saw the landmark he'd been told to look for, and to the left of the out-jutting rock face, a rock-strewn trail winding upwards. It was, a trapper had assured him, a shortcut which would cut miles off his journey, rough going, but a man and a horse could make it.

Ten minutes later he was wishing he'd given the climbing trail a miss ...

The further he went the narrower the trail became. It was a mess of loose rocks and shale, and with the sheer walls all around him he began to feel hemmed in. Snaking its way up a steep slope, narrow and twisty, man and horses were disquieted. 'Christ ...' said Dick. 'This would

3

be a real bugger of a place to be in a bad storm.'

The worst of it was yet to come as the high walls started to belly-in across the already narrow trail. Both horses by this time were snorting and blowing nervously, picking their way along delicately and uncertainly. Finally Dick dismounted, leading the horses in single file around the worst of the trail, and then there was only one wall, to his right hand. On the left was a sheer drop from the tricky three-foot wide rock shelf. Suddenly he felt sick and dizzy. Literally an inch at a time he negotiated the bend around the mountain face, and relief flooded through him when he saw the trail start to descend, and widen to four, then five feet.

He re-mounted and still at a walking gait urged the roan forward. Ahead he saw a wider-sweeping bend. The trail was now almost down to the open prairie. His clothes clammy with sweat, he never felt more thankful. Around the bend he reined-in the roan to an abrupt halt, finding the trail ahead blocked.

'Dang me if that ain't the funniest sight a man ever clapped eyes on!' he exclaimed.

Below him a battle of wits was taking place. A mule was blocking the trail and refusing to budge. A squat, stockily-built man of around sixty in grubby, worn range clothes was teetered back hauling for all he was worth on the reins.

Grinning at the welcome comic relief, Dick fished out a cheroot, lit it and sat back to enjoy the fun.

Suddenly the mule took a jump forward landing on all four feet, legs rigid. His owner, caught by surprise, fell backwards in a heap, his battered hat sent flying.

Picking himself up, then his hat and dusting that off savagely on his trousers, before jamming it back onto his head, the man stuck his face within inches of the mule's muzzle. Then he let rip with such a stream of curses and abuse, Dick was left staring in wonder and awe.

It had absolutely no effect at all on the mule. Disgusted, the squat man addressed himself to Dick. 'Of all the tarnation creatures the Good Lord done made I reckon this yere mule is the cantankeringest, stubbornest ... you know anything about mules, mister?'

'Not a thing. But carry on, this is better'n a pantomime from where I'm sitting.'

The man turned his temper onto Dick and bellowed irately: 'I've a mind to git me sawn-off and blast you and the mule both!'

Still grinning, Dick retorted: 'The mule can't shoot back, mister, but I can. You go right ahead and try your luck.'

The man eyed him with new respect, taking in the gun and strapped-down holster.

'You fancy you can wrastle that hawg-leg?'

'Some,' drawled Dick. 'Better'n you can handle that mule.'

Suddenly the smaller man grinned. 'Yeah ...

I got to grant yuh that. Now what in tarnation does a man have to do to get this dad-blasted animal to shift?'

'I couldn't do any better'n you,' Dick confessed. 'Maybe you better had shoot it and tip it over the edge.'

The man glared. 'Stranger, it might come as a surprise to you but I kinda love that there stubborn-assed animal. But you've got a fair grudge and I'm sorry my mule is holding you up—'

Another voice, from the trail on the other side of the mule cut in sharply: 'Git that mangy crittur outa my way, and let a decent animal pass.'

The square man swung round to face the newcomer. He gave vent to a further stream of ripe invective which brought a look of pure admiration to the other man's face.

'Mister,' he said. 'A feller who can wrassle cusswords the way you do oughtn't to have no trouble at all with a mule.'

The newcomer was, Dick estimated, a good four inches taller than his own five-eleven. He was thin, but looked as tough as rawhide. Everything about him looked elongated, his face, scrawny neck, arms, long-legged Levi's and tall steeple Stetson.

Anticipating more entertainment, Dick grinned. The scene was set for fireworks of an extraordinary nature. And the thought of the

6

beanpole stranger and the squat man standing toe-to-toe cussing each other was a truly delectable one.

But it didn't happen. The tall stranger dismounted and walked his horse closer.

His leather vest and plaid shirt seemed to hang loosely on him; all the same, thought Dick, this hombre is not one to fool around with.

Dick studied the tall man's horse with some admiration. A good judge of broncs, he saw that the man's animal was quality. It was sixteen hands, silky skinned, proud and full of fire.

The squat man said: 'You know anything about mules, mister? Can you git this spawn of the Devil to move?'

Soberly the tall stranger said: 'Feller it just so happens this is your lucky day. You happen to be talking to the top horse-man in the whole wide West.'

'You git this mule to budge and I'll even believe you,' said the other.

'Wa ... al,' drawled the tall man. 'Mules is like wimmen, you've got to know how to handle 'em. You can't drive 'em. You has to whisper things into their shell-like ear'oles...'

He moved in close to the mule, bent down to talk into its ear then calmly took the reins and led the mule unresisting down the trail as far as where he'd left his mount.

'Well I'll be hornswaggled!' exclaimed the

squat man. 'Ain't that the darnedest thing you ever did see?'

'It sure is,' Dick agreed. 'What exactly did you say to the crittur?'

The tall stranger grinned. 'I just told him if he didn't git the hell out of it, I'd kick his stubborn ass.'

All three laughed at that. Dick enquired, tongue-in-cheek: 'Say feller, can you handle women the way you handle mules?'

Lugubriously the tall man said: 'Wa...al I ain't a man to brag, but I can tell you men I done left me a trail of broken hearts behind me every place I've been. I'm a feller what travels a lot, never stay one place too long in case I start gitting roots a-sprouting outa my boots. So I can't afford to git hitched permanent.'

'Yeah,' drawled Dick, 'I can see you're a feller who doesn't brag.'

The squat man laughed. Then he thanked the tall man. 'Now maybe we can all get moving,' he said. 'I'm plumb sorry you gents was delayed.'

Dick was impressed by the sure, skilful way the tall man backed his horse down the precarious mountain path. The squat man followed, leading his mule, and Dick allowed his horse to pick his way down, his second horse following on behind.

The three of them had barely reached the plain below when they suddenly found themselves enveloped and half-blinded by a

8

cloud of alkali dust.

None of them had heard the distant approach of the three riders now upon them and reining their broncs to a stop so quickly their mounts reared up on hind legs.

When the dust cloud started to clear Dick saw three riders, their faces hidden by bandana masks, hurriedly dismounting. All three had rifles and these were aimed at the three of them on foot. Then things happened so fast neither Dick nor his two companions could react quickly enough to the unexpected situation to do anything about it.

One of the masked man barked a gruff command: 'Grab some sky, you three. Back off, and shuck your gunbelts, nice and easy.'

Dick and the tall stranger unfastened their gunbelts and let them fall to the ground. Their shorter companion threw his rifle down. Then all three raised their arms high.

Fuming with rage and impotence at the suddenness and chilling effrontery of the attack, Dick and his companions stood helplessly watching.

Two of the raiders mounted Dick's saddled horse and the tall man's bronc. The third hastily untied the roll on the spare mount and threw Dick's possibles to the ground. He mounted the horse and, riding bareback, joined the other two as they dug in their heels and rode off at a gallop.

Dick was first to grab up his hand gun. But he didn't squeeze the trigger. By that time the riders were out of range.

CHAPTER TWO

The tall man caught up the three abandoned horses, his face livid. He cursed the thieves and uttered dire threats, telling the world what he'd do to the rustling bastards if he ever caught up with them.

Dick fastened on his gunbelt and picked up his rifle from the ground where the raiders had thrown it. The tall man followed suit, still cursing vociferously. Lobo, who didn't wear a hand gun, retrieved his rifle.

'These broncs is spent,' said the tall stranger. 'Jeez, them bastards rid 'em into the ground. There's no way we can go after 'em.'

Dick examined the horses. 'They weren't much even before,' he declared. The tall man shot a curious look at him.

'You're a cool bastard. What the hell does it take to git you riled, mister?'

Cigar clamped in his teeth, Dick grinned. 'Oh, I'm riled. But I never did see the point in wasting energy letting temper ride me. I guess I like to stay cool. That way I can meet anything that comes.'

The old man said, sharply: 'You'd better get figuring how we're going to deal with this lot a-coming lickety-spit. Must be eight or nine of 'em.'

All three were standing close to the horses. Suddenly the bunch of riders was upon them. They just had time to spot the law badge the front rider was wearing, and then they were surrounded, and staring into the muzzles of nine guns.

Dick tensed, saw the hopelessness of the situation, and relaxed again. There were nine in the posse. Before he could say anything, the man with the badge—a fat, big, ugly hombre, heavy of jowl and with a cruel mouth barked an order:

'Okay. We've got you bastards dead to rights. Now put down your guns and don't try anything fancy unless you want to die sudden. Keep your hands away from your guns and raise 'em high.'

The three afoot exchanged looks but raised their arms slowly. The tall man said: 'What the hell do you think you're playing at, lawman? Them thieving jiggers stole our hosses and while you're wasting time arresting the wrong men, they're gitting further away. Right now you should be riding after them bastards.'

'Shut your mouth,' said the lawman. 'And don't try no tricks. It don't matter to us whether we take you back dead or alive. Now what did you do with the money you stole from the bank?' The situation was saved from developing into a complete farce by the arrival of another rider, a young woman who wasted no time showing that she had a fine temper.

She brought her pony to a halt and wheeled it around to confront the fat lawman.

'What are you doing holding up these men, Sheriff Barrow?' she demanded furiously. 'Any fool can see these men are not the bank robbers.' She turned and rapped a question at the three on foot. 'What happened?'

Briefly, calmly, still smoking his cigar, Dick told her what had ensued.

Her face red with fury, she turned upon the sheriff. 'Some lawman you are. Well? . . . don't just sit there, Barrow. Get after those outlaws. And if you don't bring them back, you'd better start looking for another job. When my father hears about this he'll have your hide.'

His podgy face pink with embarrassment, the lawman barked a command and wheeled his horse and without another word the posse rode off on the trail of the bandits.

Dick studied the young woman and saw that she was vital, maybe twenty or so, small and shaped like a miniature Venus. Her eyes were brown, and very bright, her hair long beneath her Stetson, and a mass of natural waves.

'When you've finished staring at me, mister,' she said icily. 'Perhaps you would introduce yourself and your friends. I'm Tess O'Reilly.

My father, Shamus, owns the biggest cattle ranch around here. In fact, right now you're on our range.'

Slowly removing his low-crowned Texas hat, and his cheroot, and smiling at the girl, Dick said: 'Glad to know you Miss O'Reilly. I might have guessed you'd be Irish. That's a fine paddy you've got when your dander is up. You surely told that lawman—'

'Never mind about that,' she said tartly. 'Or you'll maybe feel the edge of my temper yourself, young man.'

Dick's eyes were cool upon her and he saw the withdrawal in her face the others didn't see, a brief expression which told him, she wouldn't really care to press a fight with him.

'My name is Dick Rufus, miss. As to these two fellers, I guess you're going to have to ask them who they are. Point is, the three of us met for the first time only about a half-hour ago. Things have been happening to us so fast we just haven't had time to get acquainted.'

She nodded. 'Pleased to meet you,' she said. She looked at the tall man. Dick was tickled pink to observe the man's acute discomfort under the girl's steady gaze. 'Some Lothario ...' he muttered, under his breath. The tall man heard him and scowled. The girl demanded: 'What did you say, Mr Rufus?'

Cigar in his teeth again, Dick chuckled. 'Nothing miss. I just said I wished this wind

13

would go—'

She shot him a look which plainly said 'liar' but she didn't press it. The tall man said: 'I'm Jim Harper. It's a real pleasure, miss.'

'You're no Texan, Mr Harper.'

'I guess not, miss. I travel a lot. But if I could claim one state it'd have to be Kentucky. That's where I was born, thirty years ago.' The girl acknowledged this and looked at the small man.

'I know you, don't I? Haven't I seen you somewhere?'

'Maybe, Miss O'Reilly,' he said. 'I'm in and out of Lariat often, me and my mule. Folks mostly call me Lobo on account of me being kind of a lone-wolf sort of feller. Real name's Zacharius Grant.'

'I have seen you in town. Well, what do you three propose to do now? Lariat is six miles back down the trail from here, and those horses can't be ridden for a while yet.'

'We might as well make some Java,' said Lobo. 'I'll rustle up some brushwood and get a fire going.'

Dick crossed over to his roll, fished coffee out of his warbag, and mugs and a coffee pot. He took a water bottle from one of the abandoned horses and poured the contents into the coffee pot. The girl sat watching him and presently, she said: 'I might as well light down and join you. Then I'll ride back to town to bring out some fresh horses for you.'

14

'I could do that chore,' offered Lobo. 'I've still got my mule.'

'Leave it lie,' said Dick.

Half an hour later they sat around the small fire, enjoying the coffee. Dick, with his back to a boulder, was doing some thinking about the men who had stolen their horses. He was wondering why neither Harper nor Lobo had made any comment on the odd thing that, to him, seemed to stick out a mile.

'Miss O'Reilly,' he said. 'You say the three men who took our horses robbed the bank back there in Lariat. Did you see the robbery?'

'I didn't see them in the bank. I was leaving the hotel across the street and saw the three men ride in. Their horses, even then, looked to me to be in pretty bad shape. I saw them stop outside the bank. One stayed outside holding the reins of the other two horses while two of them went into the bank. Minutes later they ran out, leapt onto their horses. These two had pulled their bandanas up to hide their faces. Before they rode out of town, the third man masked his face too.'

'So you saw them unmasked. Could you identify them?'

She looked doubtful, then shook her head. 'Not positively. I didn't really take much note of their faces before they robbed the bank.'

Dick pursued the matter. 'If they robbed the bank they must have come out with heavy bags—'

'Oh yes. I saw the bags. Each of the two men was carrying four bags. They quickly divided these up between them before riding off.'

When Dick relapsed into silence for long minutes, presently, with some irritation, the girl asked: 'Why did you ask all those questions?'

Dick up-ended his cup to shake out the dregs of Java. 'It was just that it seemed odd to me that when those three came up on us and stole our horses, I saw no sign of money bags. They didn't have any on their broncs and they certainly didn't put any on the horses they stole.'

The girl sat rigid for an instant. She looked dumbfounded. 'Are you absolutely sure about this?'

'Couldn't be more so,' said Dick.

Harper said: 'Say ... he's right. I don't remember seeing any money bags.'

'They didn't have any with 'em,' confirmed Lobo.

'Which means—' began Harper.

'That they either hid the money somewhere back down the trail, or they passed it to another member of the gang waiting for just that purpose.'

'Now why would they do that?' Tess was musing to herself rather than putting a question to the others. Then she said: 'You see what this means? At least one of the gang must have

16

circled the town and back to the trail, while the other three pulled the robbery. And if that was the case I think we can kiss that money goodbye.'

'Do you think they got away with much?' asked Harper. Tess nodded, her face grim.

'I stayed behind long enough to learn that the bank had been cleaned out.'

'So they'd pick up plenty, is my guess,' said Lobo.

'Yes,' said Tess. 'My father always keeps around ten thousand dollars in there and there would be quite a sum belonging to smaller accounts. They could have got away with close on fifteen thousand dollars.'

Dick whistled softly. 'A nice day's work for somebody. And those hombres had a nerve, pulling a job like that in broad daylight.' The talk drifted away from the robbery. Tess was interested to know a little more about the three men she had encountered on the trail by chance.

Harper appeared to satisfy her curiosity but Dick was quick to note that the tall man didn't give much away.

'I guess you could put me down as just a drifter, miss. I reckon I've been in just about every state some time. Right now I'm headed for the border with Mexico. I hear tell there's still plenty of maverick broncs running wild down there. I'm a horse-man, not a cattle-man. And even today a man can make a good profit catching wild horses and breaking 'em.'

Watching the girl, Dick got the impression that Harper's reply had disappointed her, but he couldn't be sure when she replied, brightly and sincerely enough:

'You look like a man who could handle horses.'

'And women—' cut in Lobo, cackling into his scruffy bandana, head down.

Tess smiled and the eyes twinkled. Harper coloured a bit and shot a venomous look at the oldster.

'Oh really?' said Tess. 'Wild women, Mr Harper?'

'He's just joshing, miss,' mumbled Harper.

Dick laughed out aloud. 'Just now he was doing plenty bragging,' he contributed.

'They're both talking out of turn,' grunted Harper, sourly.

'Oh I don't know,' teased Tess. 'A man like you might handle both chores I guess.' She was doing her utmost to suppress a giggle. The moment passed and, briskly, she turned her attention to Lobo. 'And what exactly do you do when you're not in town, Lobo?'

The oldster shrugged. 'Anything and nothing, I guess. I sometimes feel like the company of others so I makes the ride into town. Then I usually gets sick of the company and I quit. Mostly I prefer my own company and the wild country. I can live off the land

18

when I have to.'

She didn't comment on this, seeming to accept it. For some odd reason he couldn't quite figure, Dick had a sudden feeling the girl wasn't just making idle, friendly conversation, but that she had a reason for wanting to know all about them.

She put the question then to him. 'I can see that you are, on the face of it, Mr Rufus, a very easy-going person. You stay cool under pressure, and there is a confidence about you one cannot fail to notice. You wear a Texas low-cut, fast-draw rig. Does that mean anything? And what are you doing in North Texas?'

Dick took his time answering. 'First off, miss, if you were a man asking so many questions, I'd not be easy-going right now. I'm kinda curious why you're so nosey?'

She coloured and had the look, for an instant, of a woman who had been slapped across her face. But she recovered her composure and said tartly: 'I am merely being friendly, Mr Rufus. But if you'd rather not tell me anything, that is your privilege.'

He grinned at her. 'You sure look mighty pretty when you're mad. Okay. There's not much to tell. I'm nothing special. The fast-draw rig ... I guess I'm just a sucker for fashion. I wouldn't want you to go getting the notion that I'm a hired gun or something.'

She gave him a hard look then, direct and

19

frank. 'I never make snap assessments of people,' she said.

'And that's a sensible principle,' he conceded. 'I don't have to tell you I'm a Texan. And that's about it. I've travelled some, tried my hand at all kinds of jobs, at the moment I'm just drifting.'

'You'll be moving on, away from North Texas?'

'That depends,' said Dick. 'On how soon I can get me another good horse, and after that, where those horse-thieves went.'

'You plan to go after them?'

'You bet I do. They stole my two horses and both are worth more than money to me. Apart from that,' he paused, deliberately, took the cigar from his mouth, and then added: 'I reckon I have a score to settle with those three hombres.'

There was no humour in his eyes when he said the last bit. Harper came in with: 'That goes for me too. The horse they stole from me is the best stallion in the whole wild West.'

Dick stowed his cups and coffee pot away in his roll. Harper stomped out the fire.

Tess unhitched her horse from the tree branch where she had tied it and mounted up.

'I'll ride back to the ranch,' she said. 'It's off the trail, east a bit, but no more than three miles from here. I'll have someone bring out horses for you. You can consider these a loan and

20

return them first chance you get. I'll be as quick as I can.'

With that she turned her pony and left the camp. Dick and Harper settled down to wait. Lobo bade them farewell and set off with his mule, heading for the town five miles away.

'Nice meeting up with you fellers,' he said. 'I wish you luck getting your horses back. Adios.'

He didn't get very far. The sound of a rifle shot alerted all three. A bullet hit the mule and he went down. Lobo dived behind a rock clutching his rifle, as Dick and Harper hit the dust behind another crop of rocks only feet away.

CHAPTER THREE

A deathly silence followed the single shot. Out in the clear the mule didn't move. Dick eased his position, lying prone beside the lanky Harper.

'Hell,' he muttered. 'This sure is turning out to be one bugger of a birthday.'

Harper grinned at him. 'Today your birthday? Many happy returns, feller. It looks like it might be your last.'

The silence continued. Dick chanced a look, his gaze taking in the rock face of the mountain now off to their left. The shot had come from somewhere over there, he was certain, and if he didn't miss his guess, from high up.

He saw no sign of life, no tell-tale movement or glint of sun on metal which might have located the bushwhacker's position. He eased back under cover. 'No sign of him. But there must be cover up there enough to hide a herd of beeves.'

'Yeah,' drawled Harper. 'Maybe we can think of some way to flush him out.'

They didn't have to. They heard an almighty yell, followed by the sound of loose shale coming off the mountain face in a miniature avalanche, and finally a long, drawn-out cry of desperation which echoed eerily all around them.

'O . . . o . . . oh . . . shit . . .'

★   ★   ★

Dick raised himself to look again. He saw the rifle come plummeting down to smash on the rocks below. Then his gaze shifted to a narrow ledge about fifty feet up the rock face. And for the first time he could see that from the ledge where the bushwhacker had been concealed a steep, shaly path it would have taken a mountain goat to climb, snaked downwards to the range below.

And down this now, helplessly, the figure of a man was sliding, at horrifying speed.

Dick was first to reach the foot of the steep, murderous slope. He picked up the smashed rifle and saw that it was a Spencer carbine.

Harper joined him, Lobo seconds after. Luck was with the falling man. Only feet from crashing to the bottom he managed to clutch frantically at a small tree growing out of the mountain face. Somehow he got a grip, and held on long enough to slow his descent. The tall Harper eased the remainder of the man's descent, taking his weight and setting him on his feet, white-faced and shaken, with his back to the rock face.

The man was long minutes before he could regain any composure. When he finally did, he looked from one to the other of the three and gasped:

'Jeez . . . I thought I was a dead man for sure. I was trying to move my position and I slipped . . .'

Harper, eyes bleak, shoved the muzzle of his rifle into the man's chest.

'You may be a dead man yet, mister. What the hell were you doing up there, trying to bushwhack us?'

Dick lifted the Colt's .45 from the man's holster and shoved it into his own belt. The man raised a hand, weakly.

'Give . . . give me a minute, hey, fellers? I . . . I can explain . . .'

'It had better be good,' said Lobo wrathfully.

'You done murdered the best friend I had ...
my mule.'

They let him sit and waited until he had
recovered. When he came to his feet again, he
said: 'I'm sorry, fellers. I made a mistake. I
figured you three were some of Barrow's men.'

Dick took over the interrogation. 'The
sheriff's men? Are you on the run?'

The man gave a rueful, bitter half-smile. 'I
am now. Barrow's seen to that ... but he's only
acting on orders I guess. But it's a long story.'

'We've got all the time in the world,' said
Dick. 'Let's move back to where we had the
camp. From there we can spot anybody on the
trail before they see us.'

He found himself being prompted by the
uncanny instinct that had served him well
during his years with the Texas Rangers, now to
take this man on trust. He liked the look of the
man. He was around thirty, five-eleven, maybe
190 lb, lean and tough. He was ruggedly
handsome and clean-cut.

They made their way back to the place where
they had made temporary camp and sat on their
haunches among the rocks.

The man brushed a hand across his face.
'Christ,' he said. 'I don't want to come as close
to meeting my Maker as that again.' He looked
at Dick. 'My name is Tim Gordon. I own the
smallest spread in Texas I guess. At least, I *did*,
until that scheming old bastard Shamus

24

O'Reilly set his dogs onto me. Right now they've framed me for rustling I didn't do, and finally got me outlawed, with a price on my head.'

The sound of a rider approaching caused Dick to halt the pow-wow, and without haste he calmly instructed Gordon to hide, and asked Lobo to position himself where he could keep the man covered without making it obvious what he was doing.

When the rider appeared, Dick was on his feet. He moved without apparent haste, yet he was beside the horse when it stopped, to catch the bridle and greet the returned Tess.

'I . . . I heard a shot,' she said. 'I hadn't gone very far.'

'I guessed you might come back, at that,' said Dick, already figuring how he could assure her everything was fine and send her on her way again promptly. He guessed it might not be wise for her to see Gordon, her being the daughter of the man Gordon had accused of framing him.

But his reasoning was proved to be awry when Gordon showed himself and started towards the girl. To Dick's amazement, she quickly dismounted and ran towards Gordon, flung herself into his arms and cried: 'Oh Tim, Tim . . . I'm so glad you're safe . . . I thought . . .'

When the two finally came apart, Dick joined them. Harper and Lobo, both looking as puzzled and mystified as Dick was feeling, moved in close.

Tess looked at Dick. 'I expect you're wondering . . .' she began.

Cigar between his teeth, unlit, Dick managed a smile. His eyes were mild, cool.

'You might say that. I take it you and Gordon here are acquainted.'

'Yes. We've known each other since we were kids . . . but there's no time for long explanations. They will have to wait. We must help Tim to get away. He can take my horse . . .'

'Whoa there . . .' said Dick. 'Where is his horse?'

Gordon explained, ruefully. 'He went over the edge a way back. I was trying to negotiate a tricky narrow trail up there. That's how I came to be up there on foot.'

Dick nodded. It made sense. But there was something the girl hadn't considered.

'Okay,' he said. 'But if he takes your horse and rides out of here, that leaves four of us afoot. How do we make it back to town, or even the nearer place, your ranch?'

'Oh . . .' It was plain the girl hadn't thought of that angle.

'Forget it,' said Gordon. He looked at Dick, a question in his eyes. 'If you three are prepared to forget what happened just now . . . I'll try to make it over the mountain, on foot. I know where I can pick up another horse safely, three–

four miles from here.'

The problem appeared to have no other solution. Dick and the others agreed to let Gordon go. He moved out to the trail to seek a spot where he could start climbing, but he was back with them in seconds.

'There's a cloud of dust maybe a mile or so down the trail. Looks like a bunch of riders coming this way.'

Dick moved out to take a look. When he returned he said: 'This could be the solution to the problem. My guess is the posse is headed back this way. If you still want to let Gordon take your pony, miss, now is the time. He'd better hightail it out the other way, at least until he can turn off across country safely.'

Tess signified her agreement. She kissed Gordon before he quickly mounted the pony, and urged him: 'Take care, Tim.'

He nodded, grim-faced. Turning to look briefly at Dick, he said gruffly:

'Thanks fellers. I owe you. Maybe sometime I'll pay you back.'

He rode off like the wind and Dick was conscious of an odd feeling of relief. For the life of him he couldn't figure out why he should feel that way. What the hell did it matter to him, one way or the other, what happened to Gordon?

The dust-cloud devolved into the returning posse, as Dick had mentally predicted. The rear man in the bunch of riders was trailing three extra broncs on lead ropes. Harper gave a whoop of delight when he saw his horse. He made a quick, yet thorough examination of the bronc and declared it to be unharmed, and made a fuss of the animal.

Dick reclaimed his own two horses, checked them to see that they were okay, then, holding on to the ropes, he spoke to the fat sheriff.

Barrow told them: 'We'd not trailed the robbers many miles before we come across your horses in a small canyon. They'd been hitched to small trees. The sign told us the robbers must've been met there by somebody with fresh mounts. We followed the trail until we lost it over a stream. Looks like them varmints got clean away. But at least we got back your horses.'

'Yeah,' said Dick. 'Thanks.' He was as sure as he'd ever been of anything the sheriff was lying in his teeth, but he told himself it was no concern of theirs, whatever the lawman was up to. He'd have to content himself that he'd got his horses back. But the whole thing stank, he told himself. And the implications of that he didn't care to think about. For sure somebody was brewing up a whole mess of trouble for somebody in Lariat.

He reminded himself of the purpose that had brought him to North Texas. Settling his own business with the man he'd hunted for so long was all he cared about. The sooner he could get that done with, the sooner he'd get the hell out of the region and be thankful. He'd had too much of getting embroiled in other folks' troubles. It usually meant gun-play, and blood and slaughter, and he felt sick to his guts of it all.

'When I'm through with this,' he promised himself grimly, 'if I come through it, I'll hunt me down a quieter sort of life.'

He experienced one uneasy moment when Sheriff Barrow asked: 'How'd you come to lose your pony, Miss O'Reilly?'

But he needn't have worried. The girl was more than equal to the tense, tricky situation. Coolly and lying glibly she said: 'I started out to ride to the ranch to have horses sent out for Mr Rufus and Mr Harper and Lobo. My horse stumbled over a rock and threw me before I'd gone half-a-mile. He ran off and I couldn't catch him. I expect by now he's back at the ranch. I had to walk back here.'

Barrow seemed to accept her story. He told one of the posse to double-up and offered the girl the free mount on loan. She thanked him and soon after the posse rode off, Tess going with them for part of the way.

When they had departed, Dick turned to see Harper in the saddle and ready to leave.

'I wish I could say it had been a pleasure meeting you two fellers,' he said. 'But I can't. Since we ran into each other I've had nothing

29

but trouble. Adios men. I'm on my way.'

They watched him go, then turned to grin at each other. Dick said: 'You can borrow my spare horse, Lobo. If you leave him in town, at the livery, I'll pick him up some time.'

'Thanks,' said the oldster. 'Ain't you heading for Lariat then?'

'Not right away,' said Dick. 'I've a mind to ride back some little way.'

Lobo looked at him, a crafty gleam in his eye. 'You're thinking what I was thinking, ain't you, Rufus? That lawman was lying about what happened back there.'

'Maybe,' grinned Dick. 'I rode that way, and try as I did I just couldn't recall having passed a stream back there.'

Lobo spat tobacco juice into the dust. 'There ain't one, not within fifteen miles of here.'

'Are you any good at reading sign, Lobo?' asked Dick.

'Man,' said Lobo lugubriously. 'I could track a blue-bottle right up your . . . nose.'

Dick threw back his head and laughed. 'Okay. Are you game? Do you mind riding without a saddle?'

'Listen, younker,' said Lobo. 'I learned to ride afore saddles was even invented.'

'Right. Mount up and let's go,' said Dick.

As they rode out, back down the trail away from the town, Lobo enquired: 'You buying into something that ain't none of your business?'

Dick turned his head to grin. 'I guess so. Feller like me can't change his ways no-how. All my life when I smelled something was wrong I couldn't be content until I'd found out where the polecat was hidden—'

'Me too,' said Lobo. 'But I'm getting too old for this kind of thing. I never knowed a time when shoving my nose into a stink didn't end up with dodging bullets.'

'Yeah. Me too,' said Dick. 'I only hope we're both good at dodging 'em.'

CHAPTER FOUR

They rode in companionable silence, each occupied with his own thoughts. Dick marvelled a little at the compatibility between them, and at the way he had felt immediately at ease with Lobo. The terrain was familiar to him and yet it never failed to arouse in him the same feelings of wonder and awe. There was an ever-changing pattern ahead and around them, on the horizon and close by. The freak nature of some of the hills and mountains affected a man's spirit, mused Dick. Sometimes he felt hemmed in and about to be crushed by these giants of nature. Other times this feeling of oppression lifted when sight of vast prairie and plain was afforded him, the lofty mountains seeming to move back out of their path as though they were trying to reassure pigmy man they meant him no harm.

'It sure is a great country,' offered Lobo.

In no great hurry, they rode close together at little more than walking pace. It was thus easy to talk, when the urge took them. 'Yeah, man,' said Dick. 'It makes a feller feel like he's being cut down to size by the Almighty.'

The trail wound its way with such irregularity to skirt the high places, a rider had to keep his wits about him all the time. It was a trail picked out by countless men who had ridden that way and pounded into some kind of permanency only by the pounding hooves of numerous horses.

Dick noted that the trees and bushes were the brothers and sisters of those he had seen in other parts of Texas, in New Mexico, down on the border, and in Mexico itself.

They passed clumps of pine and spruce, lone cottonwoods and the unexpected Joshua trees with their ghostly branches tipped by spiky brushes, reminiscent of Arizona's desert country. The wind, which seemed to be interminable, tugged at their shirts and Levi's, flattened the brims of their hats against their foreheads.

As the terrain altered, the prickly pear and yucca, in abundance on the flats, were replaced by thorny cholla and occatillo with its flame-coloured tips and barbed grey pointers. Above them dark clouds massed, hurled along the high blue sky like ominous chariots of doom.

'I kin smell rain in the air,' said Lobo. 'Dang me if that ain't strange, this time of the year.'

'Yeah. Might be a sprinkling, is all, I reckon. How much further do you reckon we have to go?'

'By my calculation,' said Lobo, 'the posse couldn't have ridden much further than we've come.'

A few beeves which had wandered from main herds now dotted the emerald green rangeland, browsing in grass that was as high as their bellies.

Ahead, the trail started to twist and dip, like a snake, and they were among piñons and oak brush. A few hundred yards further on Lobo found the place where tracks indicated the posse had stopped and milled around some.

Lobo reined his horse to a stop and dismounted to examine the sign. Presently he said: 'They stopped here for sure. There are tracks showing only three of the party left the trail at this point. Looks like the others stayed a while.'

He climbed into the saddle again and started to follow the trail leading away to their left. Dick followed close behind, himself no mean hand at tracking. Before long they were in the boulder-strewn mountains again, on the lower slopes and the main trail had passed from their view.

Lobo called a halt again after they had climbed for five minutes. Both dismounted to look at the tracks left in the soft ground between the rocks, and where the shale hadn't yet touched. They examined the sign and reached the same conclusion. Lobo put it into words:

'The three stopped here, met up with the three bank robbers I figure. All six men walked around some, then the horse tracks start off back down again, three sets of deep prints, three not so deep.'

Dick took up the story. 'And nobody else was here. Nobody met those three with fresh horses. The bandits left on foot. It looks like they made off through the mountains. It don't make sense, Lobo.'

Lobo stared at him. 'You ain't so bad at tracking for a young feller with hardly no experience. But you're right. Tracks don't lie. Those three went over or through the high country on foot. Come over here and take a look at this. Maybe they left behind a clue to their identity.'

Dick joined him and bent down to examine the boot tracks.

'See this?' said Lobo. 'Notice how two sets of tracks, the imprints is even for both feet, but the third set shows the man made a deeper print with his left foot than with his right.'

Dick grinned at Lobo. 'You're a marvel, Lobo. So we now know one of the three robbers favoured his right leg . . . he walks with a limp.'

They went back to their horses. 'Funny we never noticed one of 'em had a limp when they stole your broncs,' said Lobo.

'I don't think so,' said Dick. 'If you remember, one of them didn't move around much. The other two did all the work.'

Pensively, Lobo aimed a spit of tobacco juice at a bug crawling up a rock and hit it dead centre.

'You're right,' he said. 'Now all we got to do is figure out why they went on foot into the mountains, if there's a trail leading say, to some place where they could get fresh horses, and where the varmints finally headed.'

'That's not important, Lobo,' said Dick. 'I've learned all I want to know. My guess is that those three hombres will turn up again probably in Lariat, certain nobody is ever going to connect them with the bank robbery.'

'So what now?'

'Let's head for Lariat,' said Dick.

They rode for some time without exchanging a word. The rain that had threatened earlier didn't materialise and the sun was strong again but, now, starting on its way down to the Western horizon. In spite of his determination not to get involved in any trouble brewing in the region, Dick was, as he had always been, a slave

35

to his innate curiosity and a natural instinct to sniff out skulduggery and fight against it.

He called himself all kinds of a fool, as he had done many times before. But he knew that chiding himself wouldn't make any difference in the end.

His mind roved into familiar country, already collating what facts had emerged in the short time he'd been in the region pointing to one conclusion, that somebody was going to a hell of a lot of trouble to hide something. It didn't take much figuring out that a prime figure was the lawman Barrow.

But, Dick asked himself, what sort of prize could be big enough around Lariat, to tempt somebody to stir things up? He didn't know a lot about the cattle business but he thought he did know enough to feel certain that one man had just about everything worth money in the region, land, stock, maybe cash and property also, tied up, and pretty well unassailable. That had to be Shamus O'Reilly. A spread the size of his would be worth taking over, but Dick didn't fancy the chances of any man trying that.

He felt there had to be some other reason, if the signs he had seen so far did spell big trouble building up. It occurred to him that Lobo might provide some helpful information which might hint at a possible lucrative enough motive for stirring up a hornet's nest.

'How much do you know about Lariat, and

the range around here, Lobo?'

'More'n likely as much as you want to know,' he said. 'You want I should give you a run-down on what I know?'

'I'd appreciate it, and it might help the miles pass less tediously.'

'Eh? What was that?'

Dick grinned across at him. 'Tedious ... it means boring.'

'Man you sure wrastle them high-faluting words. Okay, roughly, this is the way things are in and around Lariat, and have been to my knowledge for the past six–seven years.'

He cleared his mouth again of tobacco juice, chewed once or twice, then continued:

'There's been drastic changes in the cattle business since the early days when long cattle drives were the thing, and plenty of acres of free pasturage for the big ranchers. Any big cattleman would have claimed at one time that cattle couldn't be raised at a profit on anything less than 2,560 acres of pasturage. When the Homestead Act was passed in '62 it spelt plenty of trouble for some ranchers. Homesteaders started moving in, with papers showing they had legal claim to 160-acre parcels of land which were only big enough to farm. Land that had been for years free pasturage was ploughed up and fenced off and cattlemen fought settlers and plenty of good men died as a result.

'But there were some ranges escaped this kind

of trouble so some big ranchers were able to keep right on raising big herds. The spread O'Reilly owns was one such ranch, and there were others throughout Texas. I don't have to tell you that ranching is no easy game. The natural threats to cattle, unfriendly Indians, also friendly ones, herd inspectors ... all added to the hazards. On a cattle drive one cowboy was needed to every 250 head, and in addition there had to be a trail boss, his second-in-command, the segundo, a wrangler and a cook. All had to be paid, cowhands getting between 30 to 45 dollars a month and found, top men more. To feed a cowboy it cost the rancher around three to four dollars a month, bacon and beans and coffee being staples.'

'So the cattle men, the big ranchers, made plenty, I reckon.'

Lobo nodded. 'It varied, year to year, and 'course there was bad years when thousands of cattle were lost. But mostly when the boom was on a rancher could figure on getting six-eighty dollars every 100 pounds of cow. Texas remained cattle country mostly because the land belongs to the state, not like some states where all sorts of rogues muscled in on buying and selling. Cattle from Texas, 'specially in the north, was usually driven to Dodge City or Wichita in Kansas to get onto either the Goodnight-Loving cattle trail or the Western.'

He ruminated for a time and Dick didn't

press him. Then the oldster spoke again.

'The next thing 'course was the big trouble when the Range War started in 1876 and as you know it only finished last year. That didn't do the cattle business any good at all. And then there was the war between sheepmen and cattlemen, mainly in Tonto County, Arizona, but its effect spreading and hitting other neighbouring states. This feud between cattle-folk called Graham and sheep raisers the Tewksburys, nigh on fifteen years of it, is at its height now.

'All that ought to give you some idea of the background to what we have left today. Long drives are almost finished with the coming of the railways and countless new restrictions on ranchers. The way I see it in a few years from now we could see the farming and business interests putting cattle-raising into a poor third place in importance.'

'But O'Reilly still controls a big ranch?'

'He surely does. I couldn't guess at how many acres range he's got. Figure it for yourself when I tell you he hires a hundred men regular and as many again for season work, extra. More'n that, he owns Lariat. Practically built the town and got people to move there. Now it's quite a place, more solid stone buildings than false-fronted wooden ones, town committee, saloons and brothels operating on licence.'

'They did that, issuing licences I mean, in

Dodge around 1870, didn't they?'

Lobo chuckled. 'They tried it, but I reckon some of them no-good pimps didn't always pay up.'

A silence fell between them again for a while. Unable to see any mental way through the mist of mystery, Dick said, presently: 'It looks as though the only possible prize worth causing trouble for is the big ranch owned by O'Reilly, then? Somehow it makes no kind of sense to me. The man must have a strong grip on everything, considering how long he's held onto the place.'

Lobo considered, then he said: 'There could be another reason, come to think of it.'

'Okay, let's hear about it—' Dick broke off when Lobo suddenly stopped and leaned from the saddle to look at tracks.

'What is it? You seen something?' demanded Dick, also reining to a halt.

'Yep, I reckon I have,' said Lobo. He dismounted, handing the reins to Dick. He examined the tracks more closely. When he was through doing this he said:

'There's fresh tracks here of a horse and buggy. The sign is more recent than that left by the posse on its way after the robbers, but the tracks the posse made returning look fresher than the buggy tracks.'

He remounted and they considered this fresh evidence. Dick said: 'That means somebody drove out here in a buggy after the posse left town—'

'Yep. And from the tracks, the buggy was turned here, somebody got out and walked some, off the trail into the rocks there on the left. Whoever it was made more'n one trip on foot.'

Dick got the picture. 'Could be the bank robbers, acting on a pre-arranged plan, dumped the money bags among the rocks. Then somebody from town drove out to pick them up and drive back to Lariat.'

'That's about the size of it,' agreed Lobo. 'If we follow the tracks left by the buggy, maybe they'll take us right to where the loot is stashed.'

'Yeah,' said Dick. 'How far are we from town now?'

'A mite more'n a mile, no more,' said Lobo.

'Let's ride,' said Dick. Then he cautioned: 'But we'd better be canny about this. Might not be too healthy to make it too obvious we're interested in those tracks and where the buggy ended up.'

They rode at only a slightly increased pace, following the trail the buggy had taken. A wild turkey ran across the trail in front of them, momentarily spooking Dick's bronc. But he quickly calmed the stallion and they rode on.

A quarter of a mile out of the town they suddenly lost the tracks of the buggy. The sign disappeared into a mess of tracks covering an area forty yards wide. They both stopped and

41

Dick stared at the confusion of tracks.

'Shit . . .' he swore fervently, shoving his hat back away from his face.

Lobo was livid. 'Dad-blast it,' he exclaimed. 'That's buggered it. Somebody drove cattle across here, and not too long ago. Now we'll never know where that buggy finished up.'

They rode on into town, despondent now that all their efforts had turned sour on them. It was late afternoon and there were lots of folks on the main street, buggies and waggons outside stores, riders moving slowly both ways along the dusty street. The faint hope Dick had held onto, that they might pick up the tracks of a single buggy beyond the cattle tracks never materialised. There were too many other vehicle and hoof tracks coming in from five different directions.

'That's it,' said Dick, ruefully. 'That buggy could be anywhere. And it could be any one of half-a-dozen on the street.'

CHAPTER FIVE

They both dismounted and walked along the street, leading their horses with one hand to bridles. Dick studied the layout of Lariat with interest. It was a sizeable cowtown with plenty of stores and gave an impression of some permanency.

About one quarter of the way along the main street he stopped suddenly, cocking his head to one side.

'Hey ... Lobo,' he said. 'You hear what I hear, or do I have something dinging in my earhole?'

Lobo, chewing laboriously at the fresh plug in his mouth, said: 'You hear it. Sounds like it's coming from the far end of the street. Shall we mount up again, go take us a pasear?'

'Why not?' said Dick with a broad grin. 'I never could resist music and the tapping of feet. Sounds like somebody's having a shindig.'

They climbed back into their saddles and rode the length of the street. At the far end of the town, just beyond where the last few old-type timber buildings petered out, they saw a large space cleared of grass and any other growth by years of pounding feet, hooves and the flattening effect of heavy-wheeled vehicles. There was a mass of gay colour from bright print dresses of the women, and some of the cowboys were sporting their best and fanciest rig. Couples were dancing and the atmosphere was lively with happy chatter, laughter and the music being provided by four men, one with a fiddle, two with harmonicas, one with a Jew's Harp. They dismounted and tied their horses to the last available hitch-rail outside a small false-fronted structure claiming by its sign to be a bar and offering gambling with house limits on stakes, carpet dice, Chuck-a-luck and a Faro wheel.

They were both caught up in the mood of the barn dances, jigs and high-spirited celebration, like most men of the West, sampling before even concerning themselves to find out who was celebrating what.

Nobody questioned their appearance and Dick found himself whirling around and tripping the heavy fantastic with half-a-dozen comely women, one after the other, to tunes familiar the wild West over, 'Fisher's Hornpipe', 'Old Dan Tucker', 'Arkansas Traveller' and 'Old Joe Clark'.

During a break in the dancing, Lobo and Dick stood out on the fringe of the milling festive crowd. Lobo asked a young cowboy, freckle-faced and skinny as a beanpole:

'What's the idee of this shindig, sonny? I ain't seen one better since the end of the Civil War.'

Cheekily the cowboy replied: 'Wa'al gran'pappy, this yere hooraw is on account today is the wedding anniversary of the boss, Mister Shamus O'Reilly. And you-all being strangers, it appears, I should tell you that all sorts of entertainment is yet to come, and after that free eats and drinks for every man-jack.'

Lobo thanked him for his information, ignoring his cheeky remark, and as the man moved away he and Dick found perches to sit on and watch proceedings as folks moved back to form a circle of space in the middle.

The fiddler stepped into the centre and removing his Stetson with great showmanlike flourish, announced:

'And now for the heddiffication of all yew good citizens and cowpokes, we have an added item. A feller who jest come to town, and he's so tall he could carry telegraph wires over a hill, is gonna hentertain with some old, well-known Western folk songs.'

He stepped back to join his fellow 'musicians', there still being no sight of the announced singer. First the harmonicas began the refrain, then the fiddler took it up and finally the Jew's Harp joined in. They played the tune through once, then, as they began a second rendering the voice of the still unseen singer floated across the cleared circle. The man had a fine, compelling baritone voice and the words of the familiar and popular song came over sweet and true and clear.

It was a song especially popular, Lobo confided in Dick, in the state of Oklahoma, and maybe originated there.

'I know the song,' said Dick. '"I'm Riding Old Paint"—at dances I've been to before it's usually the last tune played. It's a waltz isn't it?'

'Yep ... and I've heard some funny verses sung to the tune in my time, some as wouldn't no way be fitten to sing wi' womenfolks present.' He cackled, characteristically putting his chin down on his chest and shaking all over.

'I bet you have,' grinned Dick. 'I sure bet you were a randy rannihan when you were younger—but let's listen to the music.'

The mystery baritone didn't put in an appearance until the last chorus after the third verse. Everybody joined in singing the two-line chorus with more enthusiasm than tunefulness.

Dick sang the words softly, to himself, as the ballad was rendered with haunting quality by the singer:

I'm riding old Paint, I'm leading old Fan,
I'm off to Montana for to throw the hoo-li-han,
We feed 'em in the coulees, and water in the
*   draw,*
Their tails are all matted and their backs are all
*   raw.*

Ride around the little dogies, ride around 'em
*   slow,*
For the fiery and the snuffy are a-raring to go.

Old Bill Jones had two daughters and a song,
One went to Denver and the other went wrong;
His wife she died in a pool-room fight,
But still he sings from morning till night.

    Chorus.

46

Oh when I die take my saddle from the wall,
Put it on my pony, lead him out of his stall;
Tie my bones to his back, turn our faces to the
    West,
And we'll ride the prairies that we love best.

Chorus.

As the last chorus was bellowed out, the singer came from behind a cottonwood tree and slowly strolled into the centre of the revellers, singing as he came.

Dick exclaimed: 'Christ—look who it is Lobo! Jim Harper...'

'Dang me, it is,' said Lobo. 'If that don't beat all get-out. The last time we saw him he was heading south. Now what do you suppose made him change his mind, and what's he doing in Lariat?'

The musicians played on and Harper sang more songs while the space filled up again with dancers.

Dick couldn't be sure that Harper had seen them before the mass of rollicking dancers completely shut off his own view of the tall man.

'Let's mosey on around to the other side, Lobo, and when he's through singing, maybe we can find out why's he here.'

'Okay, I'm right behind you,' said Lobo. 'I sure hope they ain't too long dishing up the chow, and I could do with a drink. That feller

Harper sure can warble the notes, can't he?'

'Yeah, he's got a great voice. You know, Lobo, right from that first time we ran into the feller I had a funny feeling there was something more about him than you'd guess just looking at him, and listening to him—'

As they slowly made their way around the throng to the spot where the musicians were playing, the pleasing sound of Harper's voice could be heard. He sang more numbers, one that started with 'I'm wild and woolly and full of fleas', and other similar favourites Texas cowboys sang partly to make themselves sound tough and hard, partly to boost their own courage on a lonesome ride.

He sailed through a whole repertoire of familiar songs, all of them known to Dick and Lobo, and they were so catchy they found themselves humming tunes or singing remembered words softly as they moved along … 'The Streets of Laredo', 'The Old Chisholm Trail', 'Sweet Betsy From Pike'.

At the end of his last song and the dance which went with the music, Harper received an uproarious and spontaneous ovation from the crowd. As the space cleared of dancers, Dick and Lobo came up on Harper and grabbed an arm each.

Casually, lighting a cigar, he said: 'Was kinda expecting to see you two.'

The three of them moved off to one side. But

before Lobo or Dick could start plying Harper with questions, the self-appointed master of ceremonies announced the next item on the programme. This proved to be of interest to some of the men, to the womenfolks not at all. Six men stepped into the arena carrying fighting cocks and one character in a bowler hat opened a book and started taking bets.

The events were bloody and short-lived, one of the birds making short work of the others. More dancing followed, after which it was announced that after the final event, there would be food for everybody and whisky and beer.

The final event proved to be a mock knife-fighting contest. The man doing the announcing explained in his stentorian voice: 'We have with us today, folks, one of the best knife-fighters in the whole of the West. You all know how it was 'cos of the Injuns the old pioneers like Davy Crockett and Jim Bowie had to learn to fight for their lives with knives. But jest so the womenfolk won't go gittin' all worked up, right away I'll tell you for the fights you're gonna see today a real knife ain't used, just a wooden one. I'd like you folks to put your hands together for Yukon Judd.'

A man moved into the open space. All eyes were upon him. He was six foot, light of frame for a man his height, with broad shoulders, and a mass of hair and whiskers hiding most of his face.

Dick had tensed and become instantly alert the moment he heard the name announced. His interest in what was about to happen quickened and without conscious thought he tied the thongs dangling from the bottom of his gun-holster around his thigh.

Lobo and Harper watched Dick without saying a word, both aware that for Dick the name Yukon Judd had some special significance.

The announcement went on: 'Yukon Judd issues a challenge to any man here today who fancies he can beat the champion in a mock knife-fight.'

Four cowboys immediately volunteered, young and brash.

The rules of the contest were explained. Each volunteer in turn was made to remove his gunbelt. The challenger was then set facing Judd, each was given a dummy wooden knife, the ends of which were blunted. The left wrists of each fighter were tied to opposite ends of a thin flax rope about four yards long. When the contestants were thus bound to each other, unable to move more than a few yards away from each other, the mock fight began.

The announcer called out: 'First man to score a hit is the winner. Mr Shamus O'Reilly has offered a brand new rifle to any man who can score a hit on Yukon Judd.'

The ensuing mock fights were entertaining, but it soon became evident to men who knew about knife-fighting, that Judd was at all times complete master and might have ended each contest any time he wished, but deliberately prolonged the fights and made fools of his challengers.

When he had seen off the four brash cowboys, more volunteers were called for, but there were no takers. Then Dick unfastened his gunbelt and handed it to Lobo.

'Look after that for me,' he said. His face set, eyes bleak and with no mirth in him at all, he stepped into the space. 'I'll challenge your champion,' he said in a clear, ringing voice.

While he and Judd were being roped together by their left wrists, the onlookers cheered and called out encouragement to the new challenger.

As the announcer moved away to leave them to it, Dick suddenly took up the slack in the rope connecting him to Judd and slowly but surely pulled the man towards him. When his own grim face was no more than a foot away from Judd's, speaking his words so that only Judd could hear them, Dick said:

'I've been on your trail for more than a year, you murdering bastard. Remember El Paso? Remember an Indian Scout known to white men as Fleetfoot?'

Judd had gone rigid, his whiskered face still. 'Who the devil are you?' he croaked, shock in his voice, yet there was no fear in his eyes.

Dick spat the words into his face. 'A good friend of Fleetfoot. You murdered him and killed the only witness who could have got you legally hanged. But you slipped up Judd. The witness didn't die straight away. He lived long enough to talk to the Ranger who went to bring him into protective custody. Now I'm going to be your judge and executioner.'

'You're crazy,' retorted Judd, his composure regained. 'I've got plenty of friends here. And you can't prove anything against me.'

Dick tugged on the rope almost hauling the man off his feet. 'You spawn of Satan, you listen and listen good. When I buckle on my gun again I'm coming for you. You'd better get yourself a gun.' With that Dick released the rope so suddenly and viciously and there was such violence and venom in him, Judd staggered backwards. Then the man recovered, stood crouched and straddle-footed and, his evil face a snarl of hate, he charged at Dick.

Dick stood his ground, poised like a matador, until the man was almost upon him. Then he moved, lithely as a forest cat, turning, his feet moving less than six inches to bring his body clear of the lunging dummy weapon.

At the same instant, continuing the move, Dick circled the man at speed, half-a-dozen times until he had Judd caught in the rope, both arms pinioned at his sides.

With an almost contemptuous gesture Dick stepped in close, held the dummy knife to Judd's throat and made a show of drawing it across the man's throat.

A roar of applause greeted this, then the announcer stepped into the space to announce Dick as the winner. Dick released his wrists, shot one final mean look at Judd, then turned to walk away. The announcer caught his arm.

'First you got to collect your prize mister,' he said. 'And we have Mr Shamus O'Reilly here to present the rifle in person.'

Dick, consumed with the hatred he felt for Judd, turned. For the first time then, he realised that his brush with Judd had been witnessed by the rancher, his daughter Tess, a maturer woman he took to be the rancher's wife and a number of other town worthies dolled up in their Sunday best clothes.

He waited as the rancher came towards him with the new rifle. He saw in O'Reilly a thickset, middle-aged man around five-nine, running a bit to fat, yet still a man to reckon with, one with the kind of presence no man can miss sensing. He had thick grey hair under his low-crowned Texan Stetson. His eyes were grey, clear, and confidently steady.

'You're quite some feller,' said the rancher. 'You're new in town aren't you?'

Neither friendly nor antagonistic, Dick answered levelly: 'Yeah. Just rode in maybe an

53

hour ago. Thought the shindig was kinda to welcome me at first—'

O'Reilly threw back his head and roared with laughter. 'I like you feller. A man with a sense of humour . . . there ain't much wrong with him! I'll get this presentation done. Along with this, mister, there goes an invitation to dinner at the ranch, tomorrow night, seven sharp. Okay?'

Dick nodded. 'I'll be there. Thanks, Mr O'Reilly. It's a nice gun.' With that he turned and walked back to rejoin his friends. He asked Harper to hold on to the rifle, buckled on his gunbelt and tied down the holster. Unaware that he was being watched from across the open space by O'Reilly and his party, Dick slipped the .44 out of the holster with a slick, smooth action, checked the load, and returned the gun to the holster. Also watching him, sombrely, Lobo said: 'You did that like it was kinda important—'

'It is,' said Dick flatly. 'I'm going to kill a human rattlesnake.'

Dick was aware that the other two were now regarding him with new respect, but there was also some conjecture in their questioning looks.

'Personal business, huh?' grunted Harper. 'So I guess you'll not be needing any help?'

'That's right,' said Dick tightly. 'This is one chore I have to do myself. But thanks for the offer.'

Lobo said: 'Your personal business with the

Yukon Judd hombre—the feller you just humbled out there?'

'That's it, Lobo. Hang around. You'n me has some more talking to do later. You never finished telling me—'

Harper cut in sharply. 'I reckon you ain't going to have to go looking for Judd. Here he comes now. And he's got company.'

Dick swung around, his tough frame, every muscle in his body, and his brain instantly keyed to action pitch.

He was suddenly aware that a silence a man could almost hear had descended on the entire gathering. People were standing, like stone statues, their eyes glued to the drama about to be played out in the open space.

And he saw Yukon Judd, now wearing a gunbelt and two guns, coming into the middle of the arena. A pace behind him were three more men. All were mean-looking, vicious men with the typical cold, expressionless mien of the professional killer.

Judd stopped, twenty paces from where Dick was standing. He shouted his challenge, brash, arrogant, taunting.

'Okay, Texan. I'm waiting for you. Any time you're ready.'

CHAPTER SIX

With deceptive coolness, Dick fished a cigar out of his vest pocket, found a Lucifer and struck it on his Levi's. He held the flame to the cigar clamped in strong teeth, narrowed eyes assessing the daunting sight of Judd, with three gunslingers to back him. He knew there was no way he could back down. He'd tracked down Judd, and it had taken him a year to do it. He'd got to finish what he'd set himself to do, or perish in the attempt.

Unhurriedly he started his walk towards the quartet. He didn't see Lobo depart, hell-bent to reach his horse, but after two paces he knew that Harper was behind him, maybe one pace.

He drew back his lips in a savage grin. At least that cut down the odds. There was the same deathly, expectant silence all around he'd experienced many times. And he knew that this could be the very last time for him.

When he was fifteen paces from the four, he started to circle to his right, his body turned sideways on to present the smallest possible target to the enemy. Without taking his attention off the four, he saw Harper start to circle to the left, and he grinned. Harper, whatever else he might say he was, surely had some experience of gun-fighting.

Dick saw too, though only vaguely, that the revellers had swiftly moved out of the line of fire, and women were nervously hugging young children close to them.

Then with shattering suddenness, Lobo came charging onto the scene, mounted and carrying his own loaded rifle. He came up behind the four so fast they didn't know which way to turn, being already turned to meet the circling manoeuvre by Dick and Harper. Lobo's shout rasped out clear and commanding: 'Git your hands high, you three jaspers behind Judd. First man makes a move for his iron is buzzard meat!'

The three professional guns turned to face Lobo, now a menacing figure high in the saddle of the roan, halted with one hand, while in his other he held the rifle aimed and cocked, his finger on the trigger.

Dick tensed himself, ready for instant action, anticipating that the three men would make a fight of it . . . their breed usually knew no other way.

He knew that Harper, on his left, would also be ready. The seconds ticked away. The deathly silence a man could almost feel. Then, slowly, the three men backing Judd began to raise their arms high.

'Now,' said Lobo, addressing himself to Judd's back. 'This yere is between you and the Texan. Back off you three, nice and easy.'

It might have succeeded if Judd hadn't suddenly panicked. The man started to raise his arms, as though surrendering, and half-turned towards Lobo. He shouted: 'Don't shoot, don't shoot.'

Just for one vital instant, Lobo relaxed his vigilance. It almost proved fatal. With a lightning-fast, treacherous blur of movement a knife appeared in Judd's hand, then it was away, flashing through the still air straight at Lobo.

Lobo ducked, lost his balance and pitched from the saddle, the frightened roan lunging off at an untidy gallop. His rifle went sailing through the air to land some feet away and Lobo found himself sprawling in the dust, defenceless.

Judd started to make his draw and simultaneously, moving apart, the three men backing him went for their pistols.

Dick saw Harper make his move and went into action himself. His gun appeared in his right hand and he was standing straight and easy, cigar clamped in bared teeth, his right hand squeezing the first shot before Judd cleared leather. The man pitched to the dust and lay still with a bullet in his head. Dick saw one of the three gun-slingers slammed back, dead with a hole in his chest, put there by Harper's first bullet. Dick saw Lobo desperately rolling to get clear. Then he saw Harper go down with a bullet in his thigh. It all happened so fast it was like some crazy nightmare. Dick felt blue-whistlers tug at his sleeve and his hat went sailing away, holed by a bullet.

But he kept on firing, fanning shots too fast to count and the last two men died where they stood, with slugs still left in the chambers of their guns.

The atmosphere changed, but slowly. There was the stench of gunpowder in the air as some of the revellers began to move towards the place where the dead men lay. Dick moved in closer, made sure none of the four were moving and automatically, and with slick speed, reloaded his Colt's .44, then slid it easily and smoothly into his holster. Lobo came to his feet and moved to join him, as Harper, limping badly, and with his gun still to hand, his left hand clamped to the torn, bloody mess on his left thigh, reached the spot.

One man in the crowd urged Harper towards one of the wagons. Assisted by Lobo they bathed Jim's wound where the bullet had passed clean through, applied salve and bound it tightly with clean strips of cloth. Lobo and Jim then rejoined Dick.

People gathered around but nobody came too near, leaving the survivors of the bloody battle isolated in a space still large enough to move around.

A voice caused Dick to turn to see the rancher

facing him. The man was regarding him with respect.

'Mister,' said O'Reilly. 'I've not seen anybody so fast with a gun as you are, in years. Glad you came out of that okay. What was it all about?'

'Private business until those other three horned in,' replied Dick with calculated coldness in his tone. 'I didn't see either you, or any of your hands, or your spruced-up hangers-on, offering to try to stop what could have been me against four of 'em.'

'I never interfere in another man's business,' said the rancher. Dick ignored Tess completely when she came to stand beside the rancher.

'Shit to that, O'Reilly,' he said flatly. 'You're interested enough now it's over to ask questions.'

He saw O'Reilly's face flush a dull red, and the eyes darken for an instant, but, removing the cigar and blowing out smoke, he added:

'This was just between me and Judd, until those three gunslingers stuck in their horns. Now, before I leave this town, I aim to find out who told those three to join in. When I do find out, maybe there'll be more gun-play.'

Deliberately insulting, he turned his back on the rancher, then, as though it was an afterthought, he faced the man again, just long enough to say:

'By the way, I won't be accepting your offer for dinner. Forget it.' He turned away and made a point of thanking Lobo and Harper for siding him, and doing it loudly enough for O'Reilly to get the point and every man there who had been ready to stand around and let four men gun down one lone man.

Finally, he rounded off his remarks by saying very loud and clear: 'If what I've just seen is an indication of what this town is like then I reckon the sooner I can shake the dust off my feet, the better. It sure looks to me like a town where guts are hard to find.'

This coincided with the arrival of the sheriff, Barrow. He confronted Dick, eyes blazing with anger.

'Here's one man with guts, mister.'

Dick turned to regard the man with dislike and some contempt.

Lobo came in with an angry: 'Where the hell were you when those four were hell-bent on killing one man?'

'Yes ... where were you, Barrow?' The question was repeated by the rancher.

Dick was quick to observe the instant change in Barrow. The bluster went from the man. He was practically subservient.

Dick turned away and left the two talking. He saw a small, very skinny man dressed in black trousers, a black frockcoat and a bowler hat, appear from the throng, walking as if his legs were permanently bent at the knees, and with an odd jerky, staccato action darting from one corpse to the next and back again. He had a measure in his hands and his long grey sideboards gave his long thin face an even more doleful expression.

Presently the man stopped darting around long enough to demand of Dick: 'Who's going to pay for the funerals of these four?'

Dick replied, forthrightly: 'We're not. If you can't find anybody to put up the money, your best bet is to take what you find in their pockets, feller.' To Lobo and Harper, he said: 'Let's move. I guess I've had a bellyful of this here shindig.'

They found the roan had wandered back to where Dick's other horse was hitched and was standing there quietly. Harper had his own mount tied across the street. When they rode back along the street together, they heard the music strike up again. Dick reflected gloomily how quickly people forgot those who had been living but a short time ago, and were now on their way to Boothill. It seemed to underline for him the stark realisation of the brevity of a man's life, and the ever-present danger that any second it might be even more brief.

There were now fewer people on the streets but the doors of the big mercantile were still open. Across the street from this large building was another, set back off the street, with space for two big freight waggons in front. A printed board announced this to be Leif Olafson's

Freight and Carriage business.

'My belly's bellowing for chow,' said Harper. 'Where's the best eating house, Lobo? You know the place.'

'Follow me gents,' said Lobo. 'It so happens I got friends here.'

He led the way, at walking pace, to the livery which doubled as the blacksmith's shop. An outside forge was throwing out a red glow and terrific heat. A giant of a man was shaping a shoe on a large anvil.

'Jee . . . sus . . .' exclaimed Harper. 'See the muscles on that feller. He's as far round his biceps as I am round the thigh.'

'Yep, he's a big feller is Abe Fuller,' said Lobo.

He was first there, first to dismount, Dick and Harper following suit.

The man at the anvil grinned hugely when he saw Lobo, but carried on with the job he was doing. 'Hi there, Lobo,' he said. 'Didn't expect you back in town so soon. Where's your mule?'

'He stopped a stray bullet,' said Lobo. 'I'd like for you to meet two friends o' mine, Abe. This here is Jim Harper, and this is Dick Rufus.'

Abe plunged the finished shoe into a bosh containing water, set it down, and dropped the tongs into a rack near the furnace. He came forward and shook hands with all three. With a twinkle in his eye, and loking hard at

Dick, he said:

'It's all around town you already set your mark, Mister Rufus.'

'Hell,' said Dick. 'Then news must travel faster than us in this town.'

'It does man,' said Abe. 'In an hour it'll be in print and on the streets. I guess Pete Pollard—he runs the town newspaper, the *Lariat Clarion*—was there to see it all happen. 'Twas his daughter Rebecca come up and told us about it. But I expect you fellers will be needing to get some vittles in you. Come on, let's go up to the house and let my wife Emmy know we've got guests.'

He strode ahead of them, his back like a barndoor with muscles. He was naked to the waist and every movement he made, his great, powerful muscles performed a fantastic dance of enormous power. The sun was now no more than a red glow in the West and down the street lights were beginning to appear. The house was solid and set back to the right of the livery building. It was reminiscent of the smith, looking strong and durable, and it had size too.

Emmy welcomed them warmly, not the least put out by the news that she would have to cook for three extra men. Dick saw in her the perfect match for Abe. She was a big woman, buxom and jolly, her size in no way stopping her from moving around with energy many a slimmer woman might have envied.

64

Her home was bright and clean and her one moment of tartness came at the door to the big dining-room-cum-sitting room.

She wrinkled her large nostrils in disgust and declared forthrightly: 'Holy Mother of God, if I stank the way you three do I wouldn't live near people. Out ... OUT ... Abe, take them outside in back of the house and introduce them to some hot water and soap.'

All three, supervised in the backyard by Abe who carried buckets of hot water four at a time, took baths. Dick and Harper shaved, and changed into fresh clothes from their rolls. Lobo contented himself having as brief a tub as he could get away with and putting on the same outer clothing, only changing his long-johns when Abe insisted and tossed his soiled ones into the tub.

Dick felt, and looked, good in a clean woollen shirt, with a fresh bright red bandana knotted at his throat, clean Levi's, a vest made from the skin of some light-coloured animal, and shining Justin boots. Harper changed into all-black gear, tapered pants, scuffed boots, black shirt and vest, wearing a faded yellow bowtie instead of his discarded bandana. They trooped back to the house and passed Emmy's inspection, and nostrils. Abe took their gunbelts and Lobo's rifle and set them on a wall-side table.

By the time they sat at the big table, Emmy had everything ready. It was a gargantuan meal

65

and the four men did justice to it, telling Emmy that they hadn't eaten so good in their whole lives. Over coffee and with good Daniel Webster cigars produced by their host, they sat in comfortable chairs and talked.

Emmy cleared and washed the dishes in record time and joined them, astonishing Dick when she lit a cigar and smoked it with evident enjoyment.

They talked for a while about general topics but inevitably the conversation came round to the gun-fight. For a time Dick hedged, but finally, under friendly pressure from all sides, he told them of the things which had spurred him into undertaking his year-long manhunt.

'I was down near El Paso, in charge of a section of Texas Rangers. My warrant book lists me as Captain Richard Rufus. I had an Indian, an Apache, working for me, name of Fleetfoot. That was the closest translation we could get of his name. He was the best tracker I ever knew, loyal, and more than that, he became a friend to me. Twice, at great risk to himself, he saved my life.'

Looking sad, and staring at the glowing end of his cigar with some bitterness, he finished telling his story:

'Fleetfoot was in El Paso one day when a white man ran from a saloon, terrified out of his wits. Other men spilled out and caught him. One of these men . . . Yukon Judd, challenged

66

the frightened man to a fight with knives, the real thing. Fleetfoot stepped in and tried to stop what he saw as plain deliberate murder. The scared man wouldn't have had a chance. Fleetfoot beat Judd and took away his knife. That was when Judd pulled a second knife and threw it, killing Fleetfoot. When Rangers investigated none of the witnesses could be found, except one, the frightened white man. He talked to me just before he died in an alleyway. He'd been stabbed. Without a witness we couldn't bring Judd in for trial. That's it.'

Nobody said much. But Dick knew that their sympathy was with him. Abe, finally, after a sombre silence, made the sole comment. 'You paid the debt for your friend, Dick. And no man deserved to die more'n that bastard you killed today.'

'I guess you'll be heading back South then, and glad?' said Emmy. 'A year out of a young man's life is a lot.'

'That was the idea, when I first tracked down Judd,' Dick admitted. 'But there's no hurry. I quit the Rangers to hunt Fleetfoot's killer. Besides, one or two odd things have happened, and when that happens, and I'm involved, I start wanting to know what's in back of it all.'

'What kind of odd things?' enquired Abe. Between them, Dick and Lobo told of their suspicions about the bank robbery, and gave their reasons. Emmy took them up. She was positive, even dogmatic.

'Oh there's big trouble brewing here, for sure,' she maintained. 'I've seen it coming. And if you ask me it would be a toss-up who can trust who and who *anybody* can trust in this man's town.'

Dick's interest was immediately fired. 'Abe— did you by chance see anybody leave town in a buggy not long after the posse left?' Abe said he'd been working inside mostly that day and had seen nothing. But Emmy had.

'I did. Be about the time you say, too. It was that banker feller Mark Clayton. Now there's a snake in the grass if I ever saw one. I never could trust anybody whose eyes never look where they're talking.'

Dick laughed. 'That's a quaint way of putting it, but I get your meaning.' He glanced at Lobo. 'Maybe you'n me ought to do a bit more investigating—'

'Sure looks that way,' agreed Lobo.

Seriously, Emmy said: 'We might be needing three fellers like you three here when the balloon goes up. There's plenty of decent folk who might get caught up in it.'

Harper, who so far had done little but listen, said: 'Suppose you tell us what makes you think there's big trouble looming.'

'I will,' she said. 'Right off let me say I believe whatever scheming and stirring is going on, it's connected some way with that ranch they

68

renamed the Box G. It's been at the centre of all the trouble I've seen around here. And I've been here since soon after O'Reilly built Lariat. And *there's* another I'd not trust any further than I could throw a steer. That small spread has been a thorough bone of contention ever since it was first filed on. I've always maintained when they changed the brand they should have called it Trouble Brand, not Box G.'

Dick's interest was now thoroughly aroused. But before he could urge Emmy to tell them more, and in greater detail, there came a thunderous, urgent hammering at the house door.

Emmy leapt to her feet. But Abe was first to the door. When he opened it, now with Dick, Harper and Lobo close behind, a young woman burst into the room. She looked dishevelled, and there were black smudges on her hands and her face. She was in a desperate state of panic.

'Abe ... come quickly ... oh for God's sake before they kill him—' she cried.

Abe took her arm. 'Steady on girl. Now calm down ... cool it. What's the trouble?'

'At the office,' she blurted. 'They tried to make Pa print some wanted posters for Tim Gordon and when Pa refused they threatened to beat him half to death—'

Abe's face was like thunder. 'Who did this, girl? Who was it?'

69

'Sheriff Barrow and some of his men,' she said.

Abe grabbed a shotgun off the wall and ran out into the street. Dick and Harper were close behind, running and buckling on their gunbelts. Lobo followed at a slower pace, clutching his rifle. Harper was limping badly, blood staining his Levi's. But he'd been lucky, the bullet he'd taken in the recent gunfight hadn't lodged in his leg, it had carved a painful gash, now cleaned up and tightly bandaged.

CHAPTER SEVEN

Light from half-a-dozen oil lamps spilled onto the now dark street from the big window fronting the newspaper office and printing shop. Dick dropped back and stayed with the distraught girl as Abe led the furious race to the office. Dick saw them all disappear inside, and prompted by the same innate instinct that had saved his skin a score of times in the past, he grabbed the girl's arm, stopping her headlong flight.

'Quickly . . .' he urged. 'Is there a back way into the place?'

'Yes . . .' she gasped, breathless with the fear in her. 'This way, come on.'

Dick followed her as she raced away down a narrow gap between buildings, turned to run along the rear and finally stopped outside the back of the newspaper office, and the house where she lived with her father.

'We can get in here,' she explained, talking fast. 'This door leads into a store. From there we can get into the living room and there is a door from that straight into the print room and office.'

They went inside and through to the living room. Dick slid the .44 from the holster, checked it and pulled back the hammer. 'You stay here,' he ordered. She nodded, white as a sheet. Dick padded to the connecting door and put his ear to a panel. He heard the bragging voice of Barrow clearly.

'Back up against that wall you three and keep your hands on your heads. Snaithe, you keep 'em covered. Alder and Radley . . . get to work on Pollard. I'll teach the bastard not to disobey the law in this man's town.'

Dick didn't wait any longer. He opened the door quietly. Barrow was standing with his back showing. Rapping out an order, Dick said: 'Reach for the ceiling Barrow and call your men off. The first one who makes a grab for his gun, you die first!'

Barrow, plainly startled and surprised, started to obey. One of the men close to the man Dick assumed must be Pollard, went for his gun. Dick squeezed his trigger, shifting his aim slightly and a bloody hole appeared between this man's eyes. He hit the floor, dead before he'd had time to raise his gun. The other man close to him hurriedly changed his mind and shot both hands high.

Barrow placed his hands on his head.

Abe stepped forward and brought a big fist smashing down upon the head of the man who had been watching them. This man went down pole-axed.

Dick reholstered his gun when he saw Lobo and Harper draw their pistols. He opened the door and called to the girl: 'You can come in now miss.'

She came into the office and ran to her father. Pollard was bleeding from a scalp wound where one of Barrow's men had hit him. The girl went back to the living quarters and returned quickly with water and clean cloth and salve to tend to her father, now sitting in the chair behind his desk, where a solicitous Abe had placed him.

Barrow started to bluster. 'You'll hang for this, you four. You can't go around shooting up a sheriff and his deputies.'

Lobo stalked up close to the man, chewing on his tobacco. Then, deliberately, he aimed a spit of juice to land spat on the toe of Barrow's left boot.

'Some sheriff,' he scoffed. 'From where I stand you look like nothing better'n a polecat.'

Dick came in with a cold, controlled threat: 'You'll be lucky not to hang yourself, and your hardcases, Barrow, when the town hears about this night's work.'

'What do we do now?' asked Abe, putting the question to Dick. It was a measure of Dick's stature among men that the big smith looked to him as leader, and Lobo and Harper went along with it.

'Get the cadaver down to the undertaker's. We'll disarm the other three and tie 'em up. One of us ought to get the town committee here, pronto, for an emergency meeting.' He paused, then, as an afterthought, he suggested to Pollard, 'I reckon you ought to do a piece for your paper and get copies out on the street as fast as you can. Tell the town what happened here tonight.'

Tied helplessly to a chair, Barrow was livid. 'You'll pay for this, you can be sure of that, when O'Reilly hears about it—'

Abe crossed to confront the man and slapped his head so that it almost rocked off his shoulders.

'Shut your mouth you sadistic bastard, or by God I'll kill you right now, with my bare hands!'

Barrow was in no mood for further talk, his ugly mouth now bloody. 'I'll get the town committee together,' said Abe. 'And I'll bring O'Reilly along.'

Within the hour, the extraordinary meeting was convened. Dick, Lobo and Harper attended by invitation. They were introduced to the town committee members by Abe who acted as chairman in the absence of Shamus O'Reilly, or his deputy, the ranch foreman, Jesse Anders. Present were Pollard, Clayton the banker, Leif Olafson the freighter, John Cross, undertaker, and the barber, Kenton.

Abe related briefly the events which had led up to the calling of the emergency meeting. Then he went on:

'O'Reilly should have been here but he went back to his ranch.'

'He's not attended a meeting since the first,' Olafson reminded them. 'Ever since, it has been his foreman Anders attending.'

'Yeah ... to hand out the orders of the rancher,' said Abe. 'I think it's time we took some of his power away from him and had more say in how this town is run. Don't forget it was on O'Reilly's orders that Barrow was elected sheriff. And we all know for sure now what kind of a feller he is. I move we elect a new sheriff here and now and to hell with O'Reilly.'

The banker, a smooth character wearing city clothes cut in: 'I wouldn't do that, if I were you. O'Reilly has enough men to make dam' sure this town does what he wants done.'

Dick didn't miss the look Abe gave the banker. It wasn't friendly.

'Come to that, we've never been sure, Clayton, whose side you're on. You've only been here two years, and as far as I'm concerned that doesn't qualify you even to be on this committee. I seem to recall so far you've been solid behind every order we've received from the rancher.'

Clayton didn't bat an eyelid, and watching him, Dick assessed him as a cool, deep, and maybe dangerous man to tangle with. He didn't look, to Dick, to be the type who'd dance for any man.

'Only, Fuller,' he retorted coolly, 'because I felt those orders made good sense.'

'More like they suited your purpose,' remarked Pollard, scathingly.

Blandly, and completely unruffled, Clayton said: 'That remark was uncalled for, but we all know, don't we, that you have never liked me, Pollard.'

Abe stopped what looked like developing into a disruptive argument. 'Let's get on with the business. It doesn't matter a dam' whether we like each other or not. Our job is to serve the town and do the best we can for it. I move we suspend Barrow as sheriff.'

This was carried, only Clayton dissenting.

'Next on the agenda, we have to elect a new sheriff. Any of you got anybody in mind for the job?'

No names were put forward. Abe then offered the job to Dick.

Declining, Dick said: 'No thanks. Even if I took the job, I couldn't promise I'd not be moving on soon.'

Abe looked disappointed, but he then invited Harper to take the job.

'Sorry,' said Harper. 'Not my line I guess. I'm a horse-man. And anyway I've got business of my own right now.'

The meeting threatened to drag on interminably, things being at an impasse and finally Abe agreed reluctantly to take the office of sheriff on a temporary basis. That agreed, and Abe sworn in by the committee, the badges were taken from Barrow and his men. Abe pinned on the sheriff's star and dropped the deputy badges into a desk drawer in the jailhouse when Barrow and his cronies were locked in the cells.

The committee members had returned to their homes. Dick and his friends went along with Abe to help put the prisoners in cells. Then they all went back to the newspaper office. Dick and Harper were formally introduced to Pollard and his daughter Rebecca and they were shown next morning's news sheet which Rebecca had got out while the men were having their meeting.

Dick asked about the poster Barrow had wanted printing. Pollard showed him a sheet of paper with the details, badly-written by hand and misspelt, the ex-sheriff had demanded be produced in poster form. He read this and then passed it around. It read:

WANTED FOR RUSTLING
—TIM GORDON—
AGED THIRTY—
five-foot-eleven inches—
about 190 pounds—clean shaven—
REWARD of 500 dollars for his capture
DEAD OR ALIVE
Signed: Nate Barrow. Lariat Town Sheriff.

'Who do you think put up the reward, Abe?' asked Dick.

It was Pollard who answered. 'O'Reilly, I would imagine. He's the one would benefit most if Gordon could be removed.'

'How come?' asked Harper. Pollard, still looking pale and sick after his ordeal, explained:

'O'Reilly owns the big ranch, the Bar G, which extends from the border with that part of Oklahoma that was for many years common, free land, in the north, and as far south beyond Lariat. But there is a small ranch bang in the middle of Bar G range—'

'Trouble Brand—' said Dick. Pollard shot him a look, grinned and went on:

'Dam' good name for it that. It's the Box G. There's a story behind all this, but Abe's wife is the one who knows the history best. All I can say is that the only natural source of water on or near all that range is a sizeable lake and it happens to be on the small spread's range. Gordon arrived here twelve months ago with

77

title to the Box G. At first he left everything as it was. There were no fences. Gordon visited the big spread a lot and he and O'Reilly seemed friendly enough. The latter's cattle were allowed to take water at the lake. Then something must have happened that put an end to any good relations between the two ranchers. Gordon ran only a small herd of about a thousand head. He hired four men. Gordon suddenly up and fenced off his range which, east to west, reaches to the foothills. This still allowed Gordon access, in or out of his range, but the fence effectively divided the rangeland of the big ranch and denied them watering stock at the lake.'

'Which started trouble, as you'd imagine,' contributed Abe. 'The fence was cut a few times, but Gordon drove off Bar G hands and their beeves and mended the fence. In the end O'Reilly stopped his boys doing this. He had wells installed, some turned out okay, others not so good, but for two months now there's been a kind of truce.'

Pollard took up the story again: 'Then the rustling started. O'Reilly paid little attention to it at first, when only small bunches were disappearing. When his last round-up showed that three thousand head of his cattle had been rustled, then he hired more men—for their guns, to try to catch the rustlers.'

'But how does Gordon come into all this? It seems to me if he was stealing Bar G cattle his herd would have grown noticeably,' said Dick.

'Not if he, and whoever was working with him, drove 'em off some place else,' said Lobo. 'Point is, the Bar G foreman claims he found cattle with the brands changed. He even produced a branding iron he said was found, one that would easily change Bar G into Box G.'

Harper came in again with: 'So O'Reilly charged Gordon as a rustler and Gordon had to go on the run?'

'That's about it,' said Pollard. 'But I don't believe it. I think somebody framed Gordon, for whatever reason. Man most likely to do this would appear to be O'Reilly, only it don't make sense, a rich feller like him stooping to that sort of thing.'

'How about his foreman?'

'I don't think so,' said Pollard. 'I've met him a few times, and he seems straight as a die. Besides from the signs I've seen he figures his future is all set. He's about thirty-two and makes no secret of his feelings for O'Reilly's daughter.'

This bit of information astonished Dick, considering the affection Tess O'Reilly had shown for Tim Gordon.

'You reckon what's-his-name? Anders . . . plans to marry the girl?' he said. Pollard nodded.

'Looks that way to me. And I don't think O'Reilly would be against the match.'

'Well ...' said Dick, looking at Lobo. 'Anders may not know it yet, but it wouldn't surprise me if he had a rival.'

He didn't have time to expand on that. Before Pollard could question him about it, they were interrupted. Abe's wife Emmy came into the room having entered the premises via the back door.

'Isn't it about time you men called it a day?' she demanded. 'It's late. And we have another visitor at our house. A young woman wanting to see Mr Rufus. And she says it's mighty important and urgent.'

Dick, Lobo and Harper exchanged quizzical looks. Pollard, grinning, said: 'Oh ... so that's what you meant when you said Anders had a rival!'

'You're way off the trail,' said Dick, grinning. Then, to Abe: 'Okay, let's go find out what the lady wants—'

Emmy sniffed. 'My guess is all she'll offer a man is plenty bad trouble.'

She led the way out, with Abe at her elbow, Dick, Harper and Lobo close behind.

CHAPTER EIGHT

Tess O'Reilly was in the big main room when they arrived at Abe's house. She was sitting in a comfortable chair, plainly nervous and ill-at-ease.

She came to her feet when they trooped into the room. Dick went to her.

'I understand you wanted to see me, Miss O'Reilly?' He was formal and polite, no more.

'Yes,' she said. She glanced questioningly at Abe and asked him: 'Is there some place Mr Rufus and I could talk alone?'

Emmy started to say something, but Abe cut her short. Politely, he said:

'You can talk here. The rest of us will go through to the kitchen. We'll put some Java on. Just sing out if you'd like a cup. Dick can show you out when you've said your piece, and let us know you're all through.'

Emmy went first into the kitchen, almost choking with the effort of suppressing her feelings. Abe and the others followed. Dick said, tersely: 'Okay, we're alone. Who sent you, your Pa, or maybe your good friend the ranch foreman, Jesse Anders?' He regretted the words the minute he'd spoken them, when he saw the girl's reaction, the sudden, almost frightened, withdrawal in her face.

With obvious difficulty she replied: 'I will ignore that remark. I came here only because I'm desperate. I have no-one else to turn to for the kind of help I need. I would have thought a man like you might have understood that. Perhaps I made a mistake coming here.'

Dick suddenly found himself being affected by her sincerity, and believing her. Gruffly he said:

'I'm sorry. I guess I spoke out of turn. But this has been a hectic day for me and right now I don't feel like trusting anybody, maybe not even myself. Now will you tell me what this is all about?'

She managed a very thin, wan smile. Dick let her begin, then, after only part of a sentence, he stopped her again.

She said: 'Tim Gordon is in real bad trouble—'

'Hold it, right there,' he said. Earnestly, he urged her: 'I think the others ought to be in here to hear what you've got to say. They are all my friends, and if what you're going to ask is likely to enlist my sympathy and help then, I promise you, it will gain the sympathy of all of them. What do you say?'

She was silent for a minute or two, then she looked into his tired face and said: 'All right. Have them come in.'

Everyone trooped back, made themselves comfortable, and coffee was handed around. Then Dick said: 'Now let's hear it. Tho' I'm still wondering why you came to me.'

'The answer to that is easy,' she said. 'I saw the way you handled those killers—'

'Why do you call them killers?' demanded Dick. She was completely frank and blunt.

'They looked the type. And I know they were brought into Lariat by someone, and that could only mean big trouble for somebody else.'

'Who do you think brought them here?' asked Abe.

'I . . . I don't know. But I'm terribly afraid it may even have been my father. But let me say what I came here to say, please. There are reasons why I must help Tim Gordon, if I can. Right now it seems everyone and everything is against him. Someone, I'm positive, is doing their best to get their hands on his ranch. I don't know who is behind all this. I just pray the truth isn't what I fear it might be.'

She broke off, now almost in tears, and very distressed. Emmy, unpredictable woman that she was, came out of her seat and went to Tess, put a motherly arm around the girl's slim shoulders and said: 'Come along now, my lovely, don't let it get you down. You just go right ahead and have a good cry if it'll make you feel better.'

While Emmy did her utmost to comfort Tess, Dick looked at Abe and the smith looked at Dick.

Abe tossed his head. 'Bloody women . . . a man can never tell which way they're going to jump next. I thought Emmy hated the O'Reillys.'

Dick grinned. 'Yeah, me too.'

The two women sat side by side on the sofa,

Emmy holding Tess's hand. Recovered enough to continue, the girl said:

'I know Tim is innocent but somebody has framed him and now he's virtually an outlaw on the run. The four men he hired on at his ranch have left. And I've heard that wanted posters are going to be put out offering a big reward for capturing Tim, dead or alive.'

Abe tried to set some of her fears at rest. 'There's something you don't yet know about, Tess. Barrow isn't sheriff any more. I'm the new temporary lawman here. Barrow and three of his men are in the hoosegow right now. And there won't be no reward posters. We stopped that, okay? That make you feel better?'

The relief in the girl's face was plain to see. 'Oh yes . . . yes it does. But there's still . . .'

'The ranch?' finished Abe. He looked to Dick. 'Okay, you're the campaign segundo, Dick. What do we do about the ranch?'

Emmy cut in with some impatience. 'Won't that leave until the morning? I'm so tired I can't keep my eyes open, and this young woman needs a good night's sleep. Where are you planning to stay the night, Tess?'

'I have a room at the hotel—' said Tess.

Emmy was explosive: 'You're not staying at that home for fleas and worse. You must stay here tonight. No ifs or buts. You can sleep with me. Abe . . . you'll have to pig it with the rest of these men, for one night.'

The two women departed. Abe was looking unhappy. 'What's up, Abe, you're looking a mite upset,' said Lobo going into his cackling act.

Abe glowered at his friend. 'Aw shaddap!' he snapped. 'I'll go git blankets for everybody. And I bags the sofa.'

When he came back, Dick said: 'I'm not easy about leaving those men in the jailhouse unguarded. I think I'll go and spend the night there. I can grab some sleep and, at least, if anybody did try to break them out—'

'Suit yourself,' grunted Abe, sleepily. 'But all the windows are barred, it's a solid stone building and the doors are secured.'

'I know,' said Dick. 'I think I'll go anyway.'

Abe gave him the keys. Lobo said: 'I'll come keep you company, Dick.'

They let themselves into the building. A lamp had been left burning on the desk. Dick checked that the prisoners were still safely locked up, before he settled in a chair and put his feet up on the stove.

'We might as well have some more Java before we sleep,' he said.

When the coffee was ready and they each had a mug of it, Dick said casually: 'Have you ever robbed a bank, Lobo?'

'Thought about it many a time, the way most folks has, I guess,' said Lobo. 'Never got around to it somehow.'

'How'd you like to get around to it tonight?'

Lobo gaped at Dick. Then, suddenly, he tumbled to what Dick had on his mind.

'So that was the real reason for getting out of the house! You've got it all figured out maybe the banker picked up that bank money.'

'Could be,' drawled Dick. 'There's only one way to find out.'

'But what if Clayton wakes up and catches us going over the place?'

'He won't, 'cos he's not there. I saw him leave town right after the meeting at Abe's place. Clayton was driving his rig. It's a good bet that right now he's at the Bar G ranch, telling O'Reilly all about the meeting.'

Lobo considered that conjecture. 'Maybe. But I ain't so sure that Clayton feller is one of Shamus's dummies. I figure he's his own man.'

'That's the way I had him figured too,' said Dick. 'But I still think that's where he's gone. Already there's one thing certain in my mind about this town. There's more'n one person being devious and it's going to be a bugger of a job sorting out the truth.'

'But you're going to do it?'

Dick grinned. 'I'm going to have a bloody good try. Come on, let's go see if the town's quiet enough. Might as well get the thing done right away.'

They went out, locking up the office again. The street was deserted although there were lights still blazing from a couple of saloons further down from the bank and a few men around each of these. They moved around the place seeking a way in, meeting with no success. As Dick had anticipated, all the windows were secured and back and front doors also.

'Looks like it'll have to be roof. Take a look, Lobo. There's a raised hatch-way. If I can lever open the trap-door we won't have to leave evidence down here to show anybody broke in.'

Dick made it to the roof of the bank building in stages from a small building with a roof low enough for him to climb onto it, helped by a boost from Lobo.

In minutes the roof hatch was open and Dick dropped down onto an upstairs landing. He struck matches to light his way down the stairs and to the back door. He opened this and let Lobo in. They conferred. Dick said: 'It's odds against the money being in the bank safe, if it is here. Let's search the living rooms.' They made a thorough search, being careful to make sure they left everything looking the way it had been before they started. They found no sign of the money bags.

Frustrated, Dick swore. He'd been sure the stolen money had to be in Clayton's place somewhere. They prepared to leave empty-handed, heading for the kitchen. Then Dick had a hunch.

There was one place they hadn't searched . . .

He crossed over to the big iron cylinder stove. He felt at it. The stove was cold. It hadn't been lit for some time. He opened the top and peered inside. With a triumphant grin he said, *sotto voce*: 'Geronimo!'

He opened up the front re-fuelling door of the stove and lifted out the heavy bags stuffed with gold and bills.

Dick opened the back door cautiously and checked there were no stray drunks around. Then they carried the bags outside. Lobo stayed there while, on the inside, Dick locked the door. He left the way he had come in and with some patient juggling with the inside catch on the roof trap-door, contrived to close this so that the catch caught again on the inside.

Dick grinned. Clayton was going to have one hell of a time trying to figure out how those bags had been spirited away!

*   *   *

Minutes after, he rejoined Lobo.

'What the hell are we going to do with all this lot?' demanded Lobo.

'Let's take it back to the jailhouse and think about that. I'd like to count it, just to be sure how much there is here.'

They made the return trip to the office unseen and locked themselves in. Barrow called out from the cells.

'Hey, out there, when are we going to get some grub?'

Lobo went through and told Barrow bluntly: 'When we're good and ready. If you behave yourself you might get breakfast come morning, just before we hang you bastards.'

He left Barrow to mull over that and rejoined Dick, cackling away at his own warped jest.

Before they settled down to catch some sleep Dick and Lobo counted the money. The result was a staggering surprise. The total came to a neat, round 25,000 dollars.

CHAPTER NINE

Dawn the next day came bright and sunny but wild. A near gale-force wind made swings of heavy hanging store-signs, and rattled doors, windows and some roofs. When Dick looked out he saw that the street was deserted except for a couple of dogs scuttling to find shelter from the blow. Sagebrush littered the street and some of it was still being carried by the high wind from the range, twisting and turning, high and low, and cavorting madly before each clump of brushwood lodged and was caught in some wall chink, a door, or an aperture, or dropped to be hurtled along the street at ground level.

Lobo joined Dick at the window, yawning

prodigiously. 'It's one hell of a blow,' he said.

'Yeah,' said Dick. 'But I'm hungry. I'm going to Abe's place. You can come along when you're ready. Lock up when you leave. We'll get breakfast for the prisoners later. It won't hurt the bastards to starve.'

'What about the money?' asked Lobo.

'Leave it locked in the safe here. We'll hand it over to the new sheriff and let him decide what's to be done about it . . . and the banker.'

Outside, the wind flattened Dick up against the outside of the jailhouse. Eyes squinted against the blow, he saw a figure weaving towards him across the street. Dick tightened his Stetson thong under his chin and waited. The sound of more scuffing footsteps caused him to turn his head and look towards the opposite end of the street. He saw five men coming, heads down, battling against the wild blow.

Turning his head he saw the first approaching, shadowy figure move fast, off the street and flatten himself in a doorway just across from the sheriff's office. Some instinct prompted him then to put himself out of sight in the narrow alley alongside the office. His brain, clear and sharp on the instant, figured out the situation.

The first figure he guessed would be Harper, coming from Abe's house to fetch Lobo and himself to the house for breakfast. He'd obviously spotted the five men advancing upon the jail and had reacted accordingly.

Although it had come sooner than expected, Dick had anticipated something like this happening. He guessed the crooked ex-sheriff must have other hardcases siding him. Sooner or later they would have been bound to start wanting to know why Barrow and the other three hadn't been around. Now they were on their way to find out.

The situation, coming so unexpectedly, gave Dick no chance at all to get a warning to Lobo who was still in the office. It would now be up to him, maybe with the help of Harper hiding across the street, to make sure nothing bad happened to the oldster.

He peered cautiously round the corner, near the bottom, having laid himself prone in the alley. This way he knew, there would be less chance of him being seen. The five men would likely be looking at a man's head height, if the wind allowed them to look anywhere. He was just in time to see the first two arrive. Simultaneously the office door opened outwards and Lobo, rifle in hand, stepped out, almost colliding with the two hardcases.

There was no time then for thinking. It was all action, and in seconds that end of the main street was suddenly transformed into a powder-burning hell, with blue whistlers flying in all directions. Back on his feet, his gun to hand and cocked, Dick moved out. Lobo triggered off two shots pointblank at the two gunslingers and they were almost ripped apart, dead before they could make their play. Dick saw Lobo go sideways in a flying dive as the other three men split up, drew their guns with speed and started blasting. Dick squeezed the trigger twice, shifting aim between shots as bullets pinged all around him and spurted up dust at his feet. As two of the remaining three pitched onto their faces, Dick looked up to see Harper fire, almost at the same instant, and the last man threw up his arms, and with one blood-curdling scream, went down, twitched, then rolled onto his back and lay still.

The shooting brought people out from all directions, among them the giant Abe who came powering onto the scene clutching his shotgun. Harper joined them and briefly Dick explained what had happened. Abe spoke to the small crowd, and told them he was now acting sheriff. He ordered some of the men to move the bodies down to the undertaker's shop and told the rest to disperse.

When they started to move away, Dick, reloading his .44, looked around him. The scene was like something from a fantasy hell, with the wind tearing at men's clothing, the noise of flapping, the brushwood sailing all around them, and the stains on the street which told of sudden, violent death.

Dick slid his pistol into the holster. When everything was under control again, he checked that the jailhouse door was locked, taking the keys from Lobo.

Then he trooped off to the house with Abe, Lobo and Harper, any appetite he might have had, gone.

After a desultory meal, none of them eating much at all, Dick sought out Emmy. There were things he still needed to know that only Emmy could tell him.

Abe and Lobo left to return to the sheriff's office, Harper said he'd take a ride and spend the morning looking over the range. Tess thanked Emmy for her hospitality and set off to pick up some of her things left at the hotel the previous night.

Left together, Emmy said: 'What is it you want to know?'

'All you can tell me about the history of the Bar G and the Box G, Emmy,' he said, 'and please . . . as briefly as you can. There's things need doing this morning.'

'Okay,' said Emmy. 'You got it. The first man to file on all that range was a feller name of Matthew Grant. And before you start telling me that's Lobo's name, right off I'll say this. Matt Grant was Lobo's uncle. Lobo's own folks were killed by Indians in an attack on a waggon-train. Matt kind of adopted Lobo. I'm talking about maybe sixty years ago when all the country east

93

of North Texas was mostly Indian country and buffalo still roamed the plains around here.

'Well, Matt must have been thirty when he moved onto the range. He surely must've been one hell of a man. He established some kind of a spread, in spite of Indians, the weather, outlaws and every hazard you can bring to mind. Nobody knows for sure what really happened but the ranch did become established and well-known as the Bar G. Then twenty years ago, around the time I first came here, Shamus O'Reilly must have bought the ranch from Grant. Matt and Lobo left for the south some place.

'The part of the range that is the Box G had been settled on by a man called Ned Grayson. He came from Kansas. At this time Shamus and Ned were friendly and there was never no talk about fences going up. There was a family called Gordon came to settle in the early Lariat, when it was little more than tents and timber buildings and dust a foot-thick part of the year, mud another time. Gordon—I forget his first name—was a storeman. He opened the first mercantile. He had a daughter, Beth, who was very beautiful. The girl's mother had died a few years before they came. Shamus and Ned started to court Beth and to most folks' surprise she eventually up and wed Ned.'

'Did that start a feud between Shamus and Ned?'

'Not at all. They remained friendly, so it seemed anyway. Shamus married another woman a year after. Beth and Ned had one son they called Tim. When the boy was eight, Ned was thrown from a horse and killed. Soon after Shamus's wife died in a similar accident. It wasn't long before Shamus and Beth were married.'

'So the two ranches were joined?'

'Not really. Beth must have insisted the Box G be kept running the way it had always been and she held on to the title. She gave Shamus a daughter, Tess, and died in childbirth. Shamus was a shattered man for a long time after that. His sister moved in to bring up the two children, Tess and the stepson, Tim. The boy and the girl grew up close but some reckoned there was never much love lost between Shamus and the boy.'

'And of course, Tim inherited the small Box G from his mother?'

'Right. But he didn't have much interest in the place. Shamus kept things running the way he had while Beth was alive. The boy left for Arizona when he was nineteen. He wasn't seen around here again until about a year ago when he turned up out of the blue to claim, and take over, the Box G.'

'And since then there's been bad blood between Shamus and Tim Gordon—'

'Right. It ended with Tim fencing off his

95

range and all the trouble there's been between them since.'

'Thanks Emmy,' said Dick. 'At least now, one thing is made clear to me ... the reason Tess was so affectionate towards Tim Gordon and so concerned for him.'

They were both silent for a time. Then Emmy said: 'You're a strange young man, Dick Rufus. Why are you sticking your neck out and getting mixed up in trouble that's not your concern?'

Dick looked at her, his eyes for a moment softly reflective. 'I don't know Emmy. I guess I must be just plain dumb. I've always been that way. Never could keep out of trouble when I saw bad threatening to beat good. Maybe it was what my Ma taught me. She read the Good Book a lot and maybe that had something to do with it. She used to say "Good will prevail over evil". I changed that later on—to "Good *must* prevail over bad" ... if it doesn't I told myself, then the country would never get the chance to become a nation for good.'

'That why you joined the Texas Rangers?'

'I guess so. But I've learned one thing, Emmy. There's Law, and then there's justice, and the two aren't always the same. Depends where you are and who makes the laws. There's still only one law in the West—' He tapped his holster. 'Mister Colt.'

'Things will change give 'em time,' said Emmy. 'But you're a strange mix. The Rangers train men to be disciplined and always try peaceful methods to sort out trouble. Yet you came here, hunted a man for a year and killed him to avenge a friend.'

Dick stood up, anxious now to be going. 'The Old Testament has it—"An eye for an eye",' he said. Emmy nodded, and countered with: 'The New Testament shows us another way, the way Christ taught.'

For a moment Dick was consumed with a sudden impatient bitterness. 'Do you reckon Jesus Christ ever saw a woman and her fourteen-year-old daughter raped and mutilated by white renegades?'

Gently she said: 'No I don't think He did.'

Grimly, Dick said: 'I once came across a family. The man had been killed, cut to ribbons in front of his wife and kid. Then the bastards raped the woman and the child and cut them up. I didn't feel much like turning the other cheek to animals like the men who did this.'

'No,' she said. 'Did you catch them?'

'Yeah, I caught them,' said Dick viciously. 'I showed them the mercy they didn't show those people. I killed them with one bullet apiece.'

He moved to the door. His sombre mood passed and he managed a faint smile. 'Thanks again, Emmy. What you told me helps a lot. I'm starting to get a picture of what goes on around here. But I must go. I have things to do.'

She nodded. He went out. The wind had

slackened a bit. He made his way with long strides to the jailhouse.

Lobo and Abe were in the office. The prisoners had been fed, food and coffee being brought from the eating house, and the crocks collected and taken away.

'Let's pow-wow,' said Dick, pulling up a chair and sitting astride it with his elbows resting on the back of it. 'If O'Reilly is the man who appointed Barrow sheriff, then any time we can expect a visit from him, and he'll be on the prod. He'll bring some of his men with him. We have to be ready for him.'

'Yeah,' agreed Abe. 'What have you got in mind?'

'How many men do you think you could muster, in town, who could be trusted to back us, if it came to a show-down with O'Reilly?'

Abe gave it some thought. Then he said: 'Maybe ten, at the most. The two saloon fellers, Jakes and Penlow, and they could bring a couple of men each, Olafson and his son, Pollard and Cagney who runs the timber and paint store.'

'Can you get them here fast?' Abe nodded. 'I'll do it right away.'

Half-an-hour later, with the wind blowing near gale-force again through the town, keeping folks off the street, Abe's volunteers were gathered in the jailhouse. Dick outlined his plan and there were no dissensions.

It was still ten minutes short of eight a.m.

Dick put a man on top of every building within rifle shot range of the jailhouse, each armed with rifle and plenty of ammunition. The gunsmith, Carter, had joined them, making eleven in all.

Dick instructed them to stay out of sight, but watch out for the expected arrival of the rancher and his men. 'Be ready to show yourself if I give the signal,' he concluded.

With a reception party ready to counter anything O'Reilly might try, Dick, Abe and Lobo settled down with coffee and cigars to wait. Dick set his mind to some heavy thinking. There were still features of the volcanic situation in Lariat he hadn't yet figured.

CHAPTER TEN

With the philosophic attitude of age, Lobo settled himself comfortably and even managed to doze off, snoring intermittently. Abe seemed restless, alternating between a chair, the stove, and the small window which looked out onto the main street.

Both men seemed to instinctively understand Dick's need to do some serious thinking and left him to himself. Sipping hot, strong Java, and drawing deeply on a cigar, Dick's first thought was, 'What the hell am I doing getting mixed up in Lariat's business anyhow? If I had enough sense to spit, right now I'd be miles away from here, heading back south.'

There was no sensible answer. There never had been, with him. It was something innate in his nature to go poking his nose into other folks' trouble. Besides, when somebody stole his horses, they had kind of dealt him in . . .

He still couldn't figure why somebody was stirring up trouble. The big ranch was the only visible prize of any consequence and that made no sense at all. If, somewhere along the line, O'Reilly was in back of the scheming that was going on, it made less sense. He already had the big spread, and more than likely plenty of dinero. There had to be something else, Dick told himself. He tried going over, mentally, all that had happened. The pieces didn't seem to fit into any kind of pattern that made savvy. He considered the people he knew to be involved in some way. Tim Gordon, or Grayson, who was an elusive character. He might be up to some sort of skulduggery. But if he was—then Tess O'Reilly was in it with him. Dick couldn't swallow that. There was bad blood between Gordon and O'Reilly, but enough to warrant having Gordon outlawed to grab the small ranch?

That made no sense either. Doubts filled Dick's mind. *Was* O'Reilly the kingpin schemer? So far the only real indication that he might be involved was the seemingly scared,

100

and deferential way Barrow, at the shindig, had acted towards the rancher, and the suggestion that it was the rancher who had appointed Barrow sheriff. If this was fact, than it had to be assumed that O'Reilly also hired the eight hard-cases who had been backing Barrow.

There was something about this theory Dick didn't like. His instincts were screaming at his brain that this was a false trail, and he shouldn't follow it, if he wanted to unravel the truth. He let his thinking centre upon the banker, Clayton. Dick, at first sight of this person, had weighed him up as a man to be watched, a man with brains, devious, clever, and one who would stop at nothing to get anything he wanted.

That he was embroiled in something crooked was now proven. The fake bank robbery must have involved Clayton, and Barrow, and the three robbers who currently seemed to have disappeared. Had Clayton planned it, maybe without the knowledge of O'Reilly? If that was the truth, then it opened up other conjectures.

Was Barrow merely ostensibly the rancher's man, and keeping up a pretence of being loyal, while all the time he and the banker were plotting against him, O'Reilly?

★   ★   ★

That notion, thought Dick, might put an entirely different aspect on everything. If this was true, then the prize Clayton was after could be the Bar G.

Could it mean, in truth, that Clayton had been behind the framing of Tim Gordon also, because he, too, wanted to get his hands on the smaller spread?

This latter theory suddenly seemed all too simple to Dick. If it was the truth, then Clayton was finished and any grand ambitions he might have had, since the stolen bank money had been discovered in his house.

But then there was the large-scale rustling of cattle off the Bar G. An operation of that nature would require a lot of men ... and all owl-hooters to boot. He'd seen no sign of so many around in the town. And would a man like Clayton have been able to boss a bunch of tough outlaws? Would Clayton have had the sort of money needed to hire such a bunch?

He gave some thought to where large herds of stolen cattle might be taken. They could be driven north into Kansas across the narrow strip that was Oklahoma, or east into that state, or west into New Mexico. There were plenty of options and railroad depots, and likely buyers who wouldn't ask too many questions.

The rustling could in itself be profitable, but if that was the sole crooked purpose, how did other things, like the faked bank robbery, fit in?

There was one wild theory which might fit everything, so far. If somebody in Lariat wanted to ruin O'Reilly for revenge.

The thought prompted another question. Who would likely seek revenge upon the rancher? And one possible answer shouted for attention. The person with the best motive for such a cause was ... Tim Gordon. Instantly that didn't make sense. If Tim was behind all the skulduggery, why would he have himself outlawed and branded as a cattle thief?

Dick, his brain in a riot of confusion, gave it up. He got out of his seat and helped himself to more coffee.

Lobo enquired: 'You all through with your thinking? And what you come up with?'

Dick grinned at him. 'Just confusion, Lobo. The whole business has me baffled. Nothing seems to add up or tie-in to make sense.'

Lobo nodded. 'I guessed as much. Been doing some thinking too. Can't see wood for timber. By the way, you given any thought to what we're going to do with Clayton when he gets back to town?'

Abe cut in to answer that one. He was dogmatic about it, as far as he was concerned. 'We'll lock him in the cells with the others.'

'Don't rush it, Abe,' said Dick. 'First we have to let him convict himself, and I have an idea just how we can do it. There was something I meant to ask you Abe. At the celebration hoedown there was another woman with O'Reilly, mature woman about forty?'

Abe grunted. 'That would be the latest Mrs O'Reilly. Shamus made a trip to Kansas a while ago, met her there. Soon after she came to the ranch as a guest and stayed. They were married by a travelling preacher a year back.'

'Do you know how Tess felt about it?'

Abe shrugged his enormous shoulders. 'I've heard whispers Tess and the woman don't hit it off, is all.'

Dick pondered over his reply. Then something else came to mind. He looked at Lobo.

'You never told me you once lived at the Bar G—'

'You never asked me,' grinned Lobo. 'I never made no secret of it. Why do you bring it up now? I guess Emmy told you, huh?'

'Yeah, she did,' Dick confirmed. 'Fact is, the ranch could have been yours, couldn't it, if things had turned out different?'

'Yep,' said Lobo. 'Don't know that I ever felt I'd lost out, though. I don't think I'd have made a very good cattleman. All my life I had the wander-bug.'

From his position by the window, Abe called: 'Looks like O'Reilly is on his way in, and I reckon he's brought about twenty of his men with him, all armed to the teeth.'

Dick and Lobo joined him at the window. 'And here comes Clayton, right behind 'em in his rig,' said Dick. 'We'd better go outside to

104

meet 'em.'

The wind was now blowing with diminished force as the rancher, on a big grey stallion, halted his bronc only feet away from where Abe was standing on the boardwalk his shotgun held in his left hand at trail position. A pace behind him Dick and Lobo ranged themselves. Lobo held his rifle in both hands. Dick looked easy, and there was half a smoked cigar clamped in his teeth.

O'Reilly's men spread out behind him. Dick saw that they were not hired guns. They were ordinary cowboys. But Dick had no illusions about where their loyalties would lie. And though they would be more accustomed to punching cattle than guns, he knew also that if need be these men would use their guns and die if they had to, for the man who paid their wages.

A quick count told Dick that Abe's estimate of numbers had been close. There were seventeen of them, all carrying rifles and wearing Colt's.

'I hear you've been making changes, Abe,' said the rancher, his tone neither threatening, not yet unfriendly. Abe stayed cool.

'Yep. I guess so, Shamus,' he said. 'But I guess Clayton's already told you all about it.'

'Yes, he told me,' said O'Reilly. 'Maybe you'n me has no quarrel. But you shouldn't have acted without telling me. This is my town.'

Abe stood his ground, stolid, determined not

to be talked down.

'Maybe it's time for change, Shamus. Maybe time the town took over its own business, Shamus. Town's growed some since you started it and there's plenty folks here don't owe you a dam' thing. Besides, things are changing fast. Big ranches are going out. So will the Bar G, and most of your range will be developed, new towns spring up, maybe. Lariat will still be here when the Bar G's gone.'

The rancher studied Abe's grim face for a full minute, the jaw muscles in his face working overtime, his eyes now angry. But before he could answer Abe, the foreman, Jesse Anders kneed his bronc forward. Dick studied the man closely, assessing him. Anders was around five-ten, heavier than a man his build and frame ought to be, but it all looked to be hard muscle. The man's swarthy face was angry, his eyes murderous.

'To hell with all this gab, Mr O'Reilly,' he snapped. 'Let's do what we rid here to do. We've enough men to set things back the way they were—'

Dick stepped into the street, cigar belligerent between his teeth, as Abe brought up his rifle.

There was an audible click as Abe eased back the trigger. Dick made his signal to the concealed men on the rooftops. Men showed themselves and there came a staccato rattle of clicks as rifles were cocked.

'I don't think your hand is good enough,' drawled Dick. 'Just take a look around. Every one of you is covered.'

Anders looked around, jerking nervously, twisting in the saddle so that he dropped his rifle into the dust. He swung back to glare at Abe and shouted. 'You'll be sorry for this...'

'Shut your gab,' Abe spat back at the man. 'You never was much more than mouth and gut-wind, Anders. And you carry no weight in this man's town.'

Livid, Anders started to make a play for his side-gun. Suddenly the atmosphere was charged and electric. Dick tensed. He knew that it would take only one spark to explode the whole shebang and turn the main street into a blood-bath.

But O'Reilly came out of his seeming stupor, suddenly. He swung his own long-gun across the thighs of his foreman and rapped out: 'Cool it, Anders.'

The foreman glared, his eyes still fixed on Abe, his fingers now brushing the butt of his Colt's .45. The rancher barked a sharp order.

'I said cool it. I'll handle this.'

Dick relaxed again when he saw Anders ease off, his face still flushed and angry, and move his hand away from his gun.

O'Reilly looked hard at Dick. 'So you've dealt yourself into this, huh? Mind telling me what's in it for you?'

Dick grinned at the man, lips drawn back around the cigar. 'Nope. Fact is, O'Reilly, I might have been long-gone, seeing how I did the chore I come here to do, when I killed Judd. But before that some fellers stole my two horses—and that kinda led to me becoming curious about one or two things going on around here—'

'I see,' said the rancher. He shifted his gaze back to Abe. 'It looks like you hold the top hand, Abe. So where does this thing go from here?'

'I think you'd better get your men off the street and back to the ranch,' said Abe coolly. 'If you want to step down, you'n me can talk this thing out in the office.'

Dick moved in close to Abe as a number of things happened, then, he spoke *sotto voce* to Abe: 'Say nothing about the bank money, for now.'

He got Abe's comprehending nod, and moved back, letting his gaze rove around, as he tried to locate where Clayton was. There was no sign of the banker, nor of his buggy. It was at the same instant that he saw Tess knee her horse into view, pushing through the mounted cowboys to confront her father, dismounting and with the reins in her hand, advancing on foot.

'What is this all about, Father?' she demanded.

The rancher said: 'Keep out of it, Tess. Get back on your horse and go back to the ranch.'

Angry spots appeared in the girl's cheeks. 'I will go back when I'm good and ready,' she said. 'You didn't answer my question.' As the rancher's face twisted into a wry, evasive expression, the foreman dismounted, gave his reins to one of the hands to hold, and closed in upon Tess.

Watching, Dick was almost over-poweringly aware of a difference in the man, in his approach to the girl. Anders was a ruggedly good-looking man. Now there was a gentleness about him that was at odds with his brutal bulk and belligerent physical power. And with a tiny shock, Dick realised the truth. Anders, maybe around thirty, was in love with Tess.

Anders pleaded with her first, gentle, persuasive, but when she refused to be cajoled into obeying her father, his mood changed and roughly, he said:

'Climb back into the saddle, or I'll put you on your horse and have some of the boys take you back to the ranch.'

The girl's reaction was not entirely the predictable one at first. Her eyes widened as she stared at Anders and said: 'Jesse, I thought you were my friend—'

But Anders made the mistake of laying a hand on her, and she bridled, drew back, stumbled and fell.

In the split-second this happened, Dick moved, lithe as a forest cat. Two strides took

109

him beside Anders who swung round to face him. 'I fancy the lady doesn't want you bothering her, Anders,' said Dick, easily, almost pleasantly.

Anders stepped back a pace, an anticipatory grin splitting his dark face. He beckoned Dick to him, using both hands.

'Okay, big man. Come on . . . there's nothing I'd like better than to break your neck.'

Dick ignored Anders, stepped past him and helped Tess to her feet. They stood for a moment, her small hand still tightly gripping his, and he was wildly aware of the pulses in her hand beating rhythmically against his own pulses. For one instant her eyes looked very deeply into his, and when he released her hand, he knew that nothing was ever going to be the same for either of them again.

'Rufus . . . I'm talking to you,' bellowed Anders. Dick turned and moved clear of the girl just in time to move his chin a mere fraction, easily slipping the heavy punch the charging foreman threw at him. Reaction was instinctive. Dick hit the man with a left fist that travelled no more than eight inches, and he crashed onto his back in the dust.

CHAPTER ELEVEN

Anders heaved himself up into a half-sitting position, his face twisted into an ugly scowl. As his right hand fastened on the butt of his pistol Dick strode towards him and brought a high-heeled boot down on the man's wrist.

Anders let out a yelp of pain and Dick reached down and hauled the man to his feet. With his face hard, his eyes like granite, Dick hissed: 'You make a play like that again and I'll kill you!'

The rancher wheeled his big grey and his face was livid as he rapped out an order to his foreman.

'Climb into your saddle, Anders, and take the men back to the ranch; and move it, pronto!'

Scowling and brushing himself down, Anders remounted. He looked hard at Dick, hate and malevolence in his face.

'You ain't heard the last of me, or this, Rufus!' He turned his bronc and ordered the hands: 'Let's ride.'

The party rode out of town and Dick spoke to Tess, who was still visibly shaken, but making a brave show.

'Are you okay?'

She nodded and gave him a wan smile. 'Sure, I'm fine. Thank you for helping out.'

'Yeah,' said Dick. To Abe, he said: 'I think we can have the men down off the rooftops now Abe.' He strode into the office, ignoring O'Reilly who was still sitting in the saddle, his horse still. The rancher looked grey-faced and there was a haunted look in his eyes.

As the morning wore on, the high wind subsided and the streets began to fill with people. Abe had food brought to the office and he ate in company with Lobo, Dick, and Tess, in a silence that had become uneasy. Dick was aware of the others occasionally shooting him looks which were of conjecture, and some nervousness. He knew he had a mood on him, and he no way felt friendly towards anybody. Finally as they finished up the coffee, Lobo enquired cautiously:

'What's eating you, Dick? You got something on your mind?'

Dick turned, shifting his sombre gaze from the window to Lobo. His face set in poker deadpan immobility, he said curtly: 'Yeah, I do have something on my mind. There's one hell of a stew boiling away like the crust over Satan's kingdom, right here in this town. And more and more I get the feeling I don't yet know who are my friends and who is the enemy. I figure some of you know more than you're saying about what's going on—and I can't help wondering why you're keeping your cards so close to your chests.'

He was becoming more and more puzzled. Standing at the window he had seen the rancher eventually ride away, not out of town, but across the main street to the hotel.

And that made him wonder. What the hell was O'Reilly hanging about in town for? And there was something else. When the ranch hands had ridden out of town there had been no sign of Clayton, nor of his rig.

He just couldn't shake off a feeling in his bones that he was sitting on top of a stack of dynamite and somebody was just waiting for the right moment to light the fuse and blow him to Kingdom Come. He felt in his bones that he didn't know who to trust, not even among those supposed to be siding him.

He left the office and walked down to the bank. He looked around. There was no rig, no Clayton and the place was still locked up. On his way back to the office he was almost at the door when a fat, fussy little man came across from the hotel towards him. The man's short fat legs seemed to move with astonishing speed, rather like the spokes of a waggon wheel turning at pace. But, ludicrous though it looked, Dick was in no mood for laughing. He stopped as the man reached him, red-faced and highly nervous, and mopping at his fat face and neck with a large red handkerchief.

He spluttered out his message, fat lips ugly-moist: 'Mister Rufus, sir. At the hotel, if you please, that is. . .'

'For Christ's sake spit it out man if you've got something to say,' said Dick irritably. 'And stop acting like a bloody nervous fat duck.'

'Yes sir, it's Mister O'Reilly. He's in the hotel. He'd surely be obliged if you would step across the street and talk with him.'

Dick fished out a fresh cigar, bit off the end and spat it into the alkali dust. 'Okay, you delivered your message. Go tell Mister O'Reilly I'm on my way,' he said.

He took his time crossing the street. He found the rancher sitting at a table in the dining room, at that time deserted except for O'Reilly.

Dick turned the chair at the opposite side of the table and straddled it, resting his arms on the chair back. He studied the rancher, eyes narrowed in conjecture.

O'Reilly was slumped in his chair, elbows on the table in an attitude of dejection. He looked like a worried man.

'Thanks for coming,' he said, his voice, with its lack of enthusiasm, also reflecting his mood. 'Before I say what I've got to say, do you mind telling me what your angle is, you being here in Lariat. It might save us both a lot of time.'

'No angle,' said Dick. 'I came here hunting Judd. He murdered a good friend of mine in El Paso.'

'But something's kept you here?'

'Yeah . . . first three bank robbers stole my

two horses. I got them back, but the way it happened ... and one or two other curious things which have happened since ... we ... ell, I guess you might say I'm a feller who gets riled when his horses are rustled, and nosey when inexplicable things start happening around him.'

O'Reilly seemed satisfied with his reply. 'Okay. What would you say if I asked you to work for me—hundred a month and expenses . . . ?'

Dick contrived to hide the shock and surprise he felt. It was the last thing he'd been expecting from the rancher.

'I'd start asking myself, why? Feller like you ... you must hire around fifty, maybe more, hands. You have a foreman. You have to be the richest, most powerful man in this neck of the country. Yessir, I guess I'd ask myself, now why does he want to hire me?'

O'Reilly almost smiled, nodding his head slowly. Then he was grim again. 'Fact is, I'd want to hire your gun. Job would be to keep me alive. I've seen how you handle your pistol. I've not seen any faster, nor any cooler.'

Dick didn't allow his face to show his further surprise. 'I'd have thought you had all the protection you need.'

O'Reilly looked haunted again, just for a moment. 'Have you ever felt surrounded by friends, and yet, wondering who the hell you can trust, Rufus?'

Dick nodded. It was the way he'd been feeling himself. 'Sure. What man hasn't felt that way, some time in his life? But there must be something more than a gut feeling makes you want to hire a gun.'

'There is. I'm pretty sure somebody is trying to kill me. I've already had three narrow squeaks. I came off my horse going at a gallop. I was lucky I fell in long grass. My saddle girth had been cut through, just enough to hold for a while. Twice I've been shot at from ambush.'

'Any idea who would want you dead?'

'Only two people could profit from my death; my daughter Tess, and my wife Mary.'

'What about Anders?' O'Reilly shook his head.

'He'd gain nothing. I'm worth more to him alive. You mustn't place too much on what you saw today. Most of that was out of loyalty to me. No, Anders may be wild, and a bit short on brains, but he's a good cattleman and straight as a die.'

'That leaves the town. Anybody in town likely to hate you enough to want you dead?'

He considered the question for a time. Then he said: 'Frankly, I don't know. There could be three who don't like me, but I wouldn't have thought murderously so.'

'What about Clayton?' O'Reilly shook his head vigorously.

'No way. He's a smart feller, got brains. Since he came to Lariat two years ago we've been good friends. You saw what he did today, even went out of his way to come out to tell me what had happened in town. Let me tell you about Clayton. He came two years back. He had some money, enough to buy a ranch the size of the Box G. In fact he mistakenly thought it was up for sale—'

'You did try to sell it to him?'

He looked startled for a moment. 'Who the hell told you that?'

'Your daughter,' said Dick. 'She told me she had to step in to stop the sale and remind you the ranch belongs to Tim Gordon.'

'Shit,' O'Reilly swore, then grinned weakly. 'Okay. I guess I did try it. Figured Tim would never be back anyway. But no matter. He did come back.'

'Soon after,' reminded Dick. 'In fact around the same time Clayton came.'

'Yeah. My guess is Tess knew all the time, all the years Tim was away, where he was, and she sent for him to come back. But I've no proof of that. Anyway, I didn't mention it, but when Clayton came he had another feller with him, weak sort of man, half the time looked scared clean out of his pants. Clayton said they'd been partners in a horse ranch over to Kansas. They sold up and moved South to find land to breed good broncs in Texas.'

'What was the name of this other feller?'

'Joblin, Nate Joblin. Not long after they arrived he up and quit, said he was riding South to try his luck.'

'What was Clayton's reaction to that?'

'He didn't seem all that concerned, as far as I remember.' The rancher was silent and pensive for a full minute. Then he said: 'I guess I've been lucky, more than most men. I took over the Bar G with only a handful of cowboys, no money, and five hundred head of longhorns. It took guns to build up that spread, and to hold on to it. There were good years and bad, but I built up herds of 10,000 and more. The days of the long drives are over, but me and my hands sweat blood every year. The established cattle trails were a boon, mostly the short direct trail across Oklahoma to Dodge City.

'Early days we had to fight Indians and rustlers, later when the settlers came we had to fight sod-busters. Then they left. All the time we had to fight the weather. The Big Dry-Up killed off whole herds some places but I survived. Then came the sheep. Once we had five thousand sheep driven onto the Box G. We spread saltpetre and killed 'em off—it don't harm cattle.'

He broke off, memory dimming his eyes. Then he went on: 'When the rail depots came and the railroads it was even better. Profits were high most years—my best year was 1882 when

118

beeves were fetching nigh on seven dollars per 100lb. of meat. Yeah, I've been lucky. And when a man starts getting old he starts to wonder who, and how many, might envy him. I had three wives, all good women.'

'Why are you telling me all this?' demanded Rufus. 'To arouse my sympathy?'

'No. I don't know. I guess I just felt like reminiscing. But how about my offer?'

'I'll need to think about it, O'Reilly,' said Dick. 'But it seems to me you've had enough of ranching. Why don't you quit? You must have enough dinero to live in comfort the rest of your life.'

He gave a quizzical look. 'Funny you should say that—my third wife's been trying to persuade me to go live on the coast.'

'And?—'

'I'm going to do it, I guess. This business of finding out Barrow is no better than a bloody outlaw and thug has shaken me. And for more than a year I've been losing heavily on stock. I expect you've got the idea I still run 10,000 or so beeves and fifty-sixty hands on the pay-roll? You'd be wrong, Rufus. I've had to pay-off all my hands except those you saw here in town this morning. In just over a year somebody has run off nearly 10,000 cattle in bunches. I have barely enough beeves left to warrant employing the seventeen men left.'

Dick was beginning to have a theory of his

119

own about the rustling but he kept quiet, as he had done deliberately about the robbery money he had recovered, and his suspicions of the banker. 'That makes an even better reason for quitting,' he said. 'What do you plan to do with the ranch?'

'Times are changing. The days of the big ranch are going. I'm going to negotiate sale in sections, split the range up. I can't touch the Box G of course and that'll stay. Fences have come to stay, until a better way is found to divide up land. Even now we've whole stretches of railroad fenced off. It had to come when Joseph Glidden of Illinois, back in 1883, patented his method of mass-producing barbed wire netting. Before long now big ranges are all going to be replaced by a fenced-off chequerboard of stock farms. The whole face of the West will be changed.'

'Yeah,' said Dick, his own brain now working overtime. 'To get back to this business of somebody trying to kill you—what about Tim Gordon ... or Grayson, I believe, is his real name. I've heard there's bad blood between the two of you—'

'There is—always has been. He's resented me ever since his Pa died and I married his Ma. But ...'

'You don't believe he'd try to kill you?'

'Not the way it's been tried. He'd call me out.'

'Then why did you have him outlawed on suspicion of rustling your stock?'

O'Reilly drew a weary hand across his face. 'I left too much to my foreman. I acted on his word that Grayson was caught redhanded re-branding Bar G beeves. Same with the town business. Anders, backed by Clayton—and I trust *his* judgement, he's no mug—recommended Barrow for sheriff. I okayed it. I should've checked the man myself, I guess.'

'We all make mistakes, man. Tell me, what do you know of Judd, the knife-expert, the feller I killed?'

He shook his head. 'Not a lot. Fact is, if you want the truth, I never cottoned-on to the feller. I'd heard he was around, in town, but if he was tied to anybody else, then I didn't know.'

Dick bade the man farewell, promising, tongue-in-cheek, to think about the offer the rancher had made to him.

He had reached the jailhouse when the sound of approaching riders coming into town caused him to turn and look along the main street. The sun was past its noon zenith and the wind had dropped even more. He recognised the familiar lanky figure of Jim Harper, and saw him raise a hand to wave. Dick waved in answer. Then he saw the horse Harper was leading behind him, and the man draped across it, tied to prevent him falling off.

Abe had seen the approaching rider from the

window and he came out to join Dick, Lobo and Tess following close behind. They moved in around Harper and the second horse.

'Jesus . . .' exclaimed Dick. 'It's Tim Gordon and he looks all shot to ribbons . . .'

CHAPTER TWELVE

It was noon the following day before Tim Grayson-alias-Gordon was in a fit state to talk. Three bullets had been removed from him and he looked a sorry sight, propped up in a comfortable bed in an upstairs room at Pollard's place. His head was bandaged where one slug had creased him, his right leg was bandaged and his chest strapped-up with clean cloth.

The night before, Dick, Lobo, Abe and Jim Harper had talked. Jim had done most of the talking and new facts came to light. Soon after they had made the wounded Tim fairly comfortable but still barely conscious, the four of them gathered in the law office for a pow-wow.

'Time's come,' said Jim Harper, 'to tell you the real reason I came to North Texas. Fact is I have my own little ranch in Kansas. I breed top class broncs, three miles across the border with the Oklahoma strip north of here. I figure the way things are moving, there'll still be a big demand for good horses, maybe mostly for pleasure riding and such.'

He finished rolling a quirly, fished a match from the band of his hat, struck a light on his britches' backside and lit the smoke. 'I bought two thousand good horses from two fellers who were selling up to seek fresh pastures . . .'

Dick came in with: 'Clayton and a man called Joblin?'

Jim stared at him. 'Yep, them was the two hombres. How'd you know about that?'

Briefly, Dick told him. Jim went on:

'Yep. You had it figured right. Wa'al, soon after, a bunch came by driving maybe 5,000 head of cattle. There were ten of 'em, and they looked right bloody hardcases to me. I guessed they'd rustled the beeves but figured it weren't none of my say-so. But when they rode back without the beeves, and money in their pockets, they rustled my horses, the whole shebang. So I trailed 'em here. Earlier today I found my herd . . . in a box canyon just north of the Box G range, on the Bar G range. There were four men in there. I figured they'd not be moving before I could get back, with some help.'

He drew deeply on his cigarette. 'I cut across to take a look at the small ranch, and that was when I come across Gordon . . . Grayson or whatever his name. I brought him back here, fast as I could make it.'

Nothing more had been said about Jim's

discovery. Dick had hung around, hoping Grayson would recover and be able to tell him what had happened.

Dick had observed, with little surprise, when he gave it some thought, the great concern Rebecca Pollard had shown for Tim Grayson. She had hardly left his bedside. He figured the two had something good going between them. He hoped fervently the man survived to enjoy the fruits of their evident affection for each other, although, truth to tell, Tim hadn't been in a fit state to show it much as yet. Tess had stayed at the house also to help out, and his own thoughts concerning her were a riot of emotion-stirring ones.

Before grabbing some sleep that previous night, he'd gone over the new events and information gleaned, and he began to see a glimmer of sense stealing in, helping him sort out some of the intrigue and mystery, at least ... to make some good guesses, which he'd not been able to do before.

He was with the others, at Tim's bedside, when the young man talked. He looked rough, thought Dick, like death warmed up. The man had been lucky, and for sure he was one tough fighter.

Tim, weakly, told them what had happened: 'I'd been hiding out in the foothills, now and then riding out to keep an eye on my ranch. Until yesterday everything had looked quiet, nobody around, nobody trying to take over, my fences intact. Then, yesterday I rode slap bang into trouble. Christ ... the locals sure named that bloody place right when they called it Trouble Brand ... there were eight hardcases—three at the ranch house, three putting up fresh fence posts and barbed wire netting to cut off the water-hole. The other two were starting to cut a gap in the main fence dividing my range from O'Reilly's.'

He paused, breathing with difficulty, so that Dick was prompted to urge him to take it easy. But he went on:

'They spotted me. I found cover but they flushed me out and I thought I was a goner. I reckon they must have seen Jim Harper coming and then left me to die. That's it.'

Tess, full of concern, said: 'But what's to happen to your ranch? We can't let those men, whoever they are, take over—'

Grimly, Dick assured her: 'We won't. I have an idea. You're not going to be in any shape to do much about it for some time, Tim. Will you trust me?'

'From what Tess has told me ... with my life, Dick,' he said.

Dick outlined his plan. 'Sign a Bill of Sale making me owner of your Trouble Brand. I'll do my best to hold on to it until you're on your feet again.'

This was done, Abe and Tess signing as

witnesses to the mock sale, and Dick pocketed the document. 'Now . . . we don't want to over-tire you, but there's one more thing you might help clear up.'

He told Tim about the bank robbery, what he and Lobo had discovered, and how they had recovered the cash from Clayton's place. 'We counted the dinero,' he said. 'It comes to 25,000 dollars.'

Tim whistled softly. 'I don't know about the rest of it but 10,000 dollars of that is mine. I lodged it at the bank against buying in stock when I got around to it—they never gave me a chance to. I would guess O'Reilly put the remainder in.'

'O'Reilly put in the same amount as you,' Dick corrected. 'The rest must belong to small investors. Thing is, until we get this business sorted out, I think we'll move the money from the safe in the office and hide it somewhere else. Anybody got any ideas?'

'Why not hide it here at Pollard's place?' suggested Abe.

It was agreed and the money was carted there, everybody lending a hand to make the switch. They left Tim then to get some rest, with Rebecca at his bedside. Dick took Tess to one side.

'There's some information you might be able to give me, Tess,' he said. 'I just want to check something I learned elsewhere. Do you mind?'

She shook her head. 'Anything I can do to help, Dick.'

'When Tim . . . he's your step-brother isn't he? . . . left the region some years ago, did you know where he was going?'

She nodded. 'Yes. As children we were very close. I knew he hated my father, and never got over his father's death. We made a pact to keep in touch.'

'And it was you who sent for Tim when your Pa tried to sell the small spread?'

'Yes. There was a fearful row. I never liked my Pa's new wife. I still don't. I've nothing really to go on but I never trusted her. I think she made a play for Pa from the time she came as a guest, from Kansas, where Pa met her. About Tim and me, yes, he is my half-brother. Beth was his mother, his Pa was Grayson. Beth was my mother when she later married Pa. There . . . is something else . . . I don't know if it might be just that I dislike my new step-mother . . .'

'Come on . . . let's hear it. Anything might help me unravel what's going on around here.'

Hesitantly, as if not sure of herself, she said: 'When she first came to the ranch, her name by the way was Mary Carter . . . she claimed that she was a life-long friend of my late mother Beth. She said they had grown up together as children back in Kansas. Mary met and married a Union Army Officer and for a time they went

127

to live in Canada. When her first husband died she returned to her former home in Kansas. I now believe she deliberately found out my mother was dead and that she sought out ... fixed to meet Pa on one of his visits to Kansas on business.'

Dick pondered over this fresh information. He thanked her, and then, gruffly, said: 'I've work to do. It's going to be dangerous. But when this is all over, if I come through it ...'

She gazed steadily into his eyes. 'Yes ...' she whispered.

He was suddenly embarrassed. 'Oh hell ...' he said. 'You know what I mean.'

She reached up and kissed his cheek, her eyes sparkling mischievously. 'Yes,' she said softly. 'I know what you mean. And please be careful Dick. I *want* to hear you finish saying what you just started ...'

He made his way back to the jailhouse and rejoined the other three. He drank some hot black Java and mulled over the new facts he had learned.

Three men had pulled a fake robbery. Ostensibly, they'd ridden a long way on horses that were so blown they'd had to steal others, his own and Jim Harper's. The cash had been picked up in Clayton's buggy and found hidden in the man's back-room stove. It looked open and shut that Clayton had been in on the fake bank robbery, which meant he had paid the robbers to do it. They needn't have ridden from a distance. The blown horses could have been rigged, just to make it look that way. And the ex-sheriff, Barrow, had been involved in the set-up robbery. But why?

What had been the purpose of the fake robbery? Clayton looked as guilty as all get out—and yet somebody could have set *him* up. Somebody else could have used the rig and hidden the money at banker Clayton's place? O'Reilly clearly didn't know it had been a fake job, and he swore by Clayton's honesty.

And how did all this fit in with the evident desire of somebody, for some reason, to get their hands on Trouble Brand ... the Box G? The pieces still didn't seem to fit together to make sense or logic. O'Reilly had no crooked axe to grind, on the face of it. He was getting out anyway, quitting ranching for the easy life. Tim Grayson, it seemed, was only concerned about hanging on to what was his—he didn't appear to know why his ranch was so important. At least, if he did, he wasn't saying.

Who the hell was fighting who? And who was on which side? How many bloody sides were there?

The one important pointer that had come out so far was the part Judd had played. The man he had murdered back in El Paso had been Joblin. And Joblin had before that come to Lariat as Clayton's partner. Why had he left and headed

South? And why had Judd been sent after him, to kill him? To shut his mouth, stop him blabbing something he knew about what was afoot in Lariat?

Dick gave it up for the time, aware at least that whatever had been going on, for some time now, in Lariat, had been connected with the murder of the man he'd come to avenge, and Joblin. But now there were things to be done, and urgently. He was further delayed, putting his next plan into action by the arrival at the office of Rebecca.

'Can you come?' she asked. 'It's Tim. He wants to talk to you, Dick, alone.'

Dick made his way to the house. What Tim Grayson told him, privately, came as a bombshell. It was a possibility that had never occurred to Dick.

'I want you to take this as I did, for what it's worth,' confided Tim. 'And when you hear what I'm going to tell you, you'll know why I didn't want to say anything to the others. I've not even talked about this to Tess. Fact is, just before you arrived here, O'Reilly's new wife spoke to me at the hotel here, just before they— *somebody*—tried to frame me for rustling. She told me she suspected O'Reilly had engineered the death of Grayson, my Pa ... cut through his saddle girth so he fell and was killed. She went further ... hinting that he'd always wanted Beth and after killing my Pa, he murdered his first wife.'

The news left Dick feeling shattered. 'Now why in God's name would she do a thing like that? She told you these things, yet she had married O'Reilly . . . what was your reaction?'

'Pretty much the same as yours is now. She warned me, then, that O'Reilly might be planning to kill me too and hinted that it might be wiser if I left. Then she made me an offer for the Box G.'

Stunned, Dick didn't know what to say. The woman's move looked to be a fool one at best. For Christ's sake what was her motive? And how much truth was there in her wild accusations concerning the rancher?

'Yeah . . . kind of shakes you don't it?' said Tim. 'You see how smart she was though? She knew dam' well I couldn't go to O'Reilly and tell him what she'd said. She knew O'Reilly and me were at outs, and anyway he'd never have believed me, even if I could have told him.'

'Yeah,' said Dick. 'I can see that . . . so, whatever her motive, she had nothing to lose. She could always have denied saying these things to you. But you told her, in no uncertain manner, that you weren't selling?'

'Right. Keep this to yourself. If it helps you get to the bottom of what's going on around here, okay. But don't tell anybody else.'

'I won't . . . at least not yet,' promised Dick. 'I'm going out to your ranch now, taking Lobo and Jim Harper with me. Take care of yourself.'

A mile from the small ranch, Dick, Lobo and Jim met seven of the Bar G cowboys riding towards Lariat. Dick talked to the front man. 'Howdi, fellers,' he greeted. 'Where you heading?'

'Any place and no place, I guess,' said the cowboy. 'You see before you seven unemployed cowhands. We just got fired.'

'Like to tell us about it?' said Dick.

'Why not?' drawled the hand. 'We'd rounded up what was left of the beeves, druv 'em to the home range. They's maybe three-to-four hundred left. Then, couple hours back, the boss's lady came out to pay us all off, and we was told the ranch is being sold off in section lots. We had an idea something of the sort was in the wind so it didn't come as any big surprise.'

'What about the other cowboys?'

'Oh they done hit the breeze every which-way, north south east or west to seek jobs. We figured we'd have us a long lonesome in town, spend what we've got and git drunk a bit, afore we move on, maybe south.'

Dick considered. An idea came to mind. Impulsively, he said: 'How'd you fellers like to work for me? I've just bought the Box G and I'm going to need some hands.'

The cowboy studied him, seriously. 'That the truth, mister? Way I heard it Tim Gordon wouldn't sell at any price.'

Dick fished out the Bill of Sale and showed it. Convinced, the hand talked it over with the others. Then he said:

'Mister, you just hired yourself seven cowboys. Only one favour we ask. First we'd like to go git us a drink, maybe two. Suit you?'

'Okay,' Dick agreed. 'I'll expect you at the ranch later. Just one thing, don't turn up drunk. And there might be gun-play, so if any of you don't fancy laying your skins on the line with the job, better not come back. Be seeing you, men.'

The cowboys proceeded on their way to town. Dick and his companions veered off the trail to the big ranch, heading towards the Box G. In the last of the foothills where there was still cover, they called a halt.

'I figure we're about a halfmile from the ranch house,' said Dick. 'Let's take a look ahead.'

He took field-glasses from his saddle roll and settled behind a boulder on which he could rest his elbows, he focussed on the line of fence. When he had a spot some hundreds of yards away in view, he passed the glasses to Lobo, who took a look and handed them to Jim who in turn took a look.

'Two of 'em,' said Dick. 'Looks like they've taken down maybe fifty yards of fencing and moving along this way.'

'What are we going to do?' asked Jim. Dick

grinned, lighting a cigar.

'Make 'em put it up again. Come on, let's ride.'

They came up on the two men, surprising them, and quickly disarmed them. Dick wasted no time explaining to them what was going on. He left Lobo to cover them with his rifle and make sure they did the repair job.

'We'll take their horses on up to the ranch with us,' he said. 'When you two have finished the job you can walk back to the house to collect your broncs.'

He rode away, leaving the two men mouthing obscenities, Jim close behind him. When they were within sight of the house and the water close by, Dick reined in again.

'I'm going to ride straight on up to the lake, Jim,' he said. 'How about you making a wide circle to come up behind, between the men at the water, and the house—only watch your back.'

'You got it,' said Jim. He rode away at a gallop.

Dick continued his approach at a more leisurely gait, allowing Jim time to circle around behind the lake. He was almost upon the men erecting new, high barbed wire fencing around the water before they spotted him. Then one of them moved out, on foot, to confront Dick, as he stopped and dismounted, trailing his mount's reins, and those of the other two horses to prevent them straying far. He saw the man peel off his heavy gloves and advance, right hand on his gun.

CHAPTER THIRTEEN

Dick adopted a casual attitude, deceptive, but he was keyed, ready, to the pitch for instant deadly action, if the other man made his play.

'What the hell are you doing on this land?' the man demanded. 'You're trespassing.'

Dick grinned around the cigar clamped in his teeth. 'You got that all wrong mister. You're the one trespassing. I'm the new owner of this spread. Now what the hell are you doing, fencing off my lake?'

The man's face twisted, and his eyes narrowed, to Dick a dead give away, even before he started to pull the pistol from his holster. Dick drew his own gun effortlessly, with eye-defying speed and squeezed off one shot. A bloody, gashed hole appeared between the man's eyes and with a shocked, silently-screaming open mouth, he fell dead at Dick's feet.

The gun-play brought the other three working on the fence, running, desperately tearing off their gloves and grabbing for their irons. Dick calmly fired, fanning the trigger,

135

shooting from his hip, and one after the other, the three pitched onto their faces, only one writhing and screaming agony before he too died in the mud around the lake.

Reloading, and sliding the Colt's back into the holster, Dick muttered: 'Damnation. I figured on making the bastards take down that fence—'

He saw Jim across the narrow strip of the lake, behind him the small, neat ranch house. He watched Jim dismount, tie his horse to a lake-side sapling and walk to the edge of the water. He called across: 'Man you're a devil on two legs with that hawg's leg ... you coming on?'

'Yeah ... I'm coming,' Dick called back. He retrieved his own horse, mounted and skirting the edge of the lake, rode to join Jim, some two hundred yards from the house.

He dismounted and tied his bronc alongside Jim's. As they set off towards the house, they saw four figures emerge, mount horses and come riding slowly towards them.

The front rider was Mary O'Reilly. Behind her rode the last three hardcases.

Dick stopped and stood his ground, nerves keened and alert, with Jim at his side also ready to go into action.

But there was no more shooting. The woman was handsome, cool and composed. She looked about forty, and sat her small black stallion like a man. Dressed all in black, with a low-crowned, wide-brimmed feminine Texas-style Stetson, she made an impressive picture. In her face was a haughtiness. In her dark eyes, an odd kind of serenity. When she stopped her horse yards from where he stood, Dick touched his hat, but he didn't remove the cigar from his teeth.

'Ma'am,' he said. 'I'd be obliged if you would tell me what you and your men ... I take it these ornery-looking bastards are working for you? ... are doing on my land.'

'*Your* land, sir?' she countered.

Dick fished the Bill of Sale from his pocket. 'This here piece of paper gives me title, ma'am. I just bought the spread from Mr Tim Gordon.'

'May I see that?' she asked. Dick stepped close.

He held on to the document while she leaned over to peruse it. When she straightened up again she had a sardonic smile on her narrow lips.

'The paper would seem to support your claim. How did you manage it? What peculiar kind of magic did you exert to persuade Gordon ... that is, Grayson ... to sell?'

'No magic, ma'am,' said Dick levelly. 'Now if you would oblige me? Just what the hell are you doing on my land, and why are your men fencing off my lake?'

For a moment she appeared to be nonplussed,

even temporarily at a loss for words. But the moment didn't last. Cool as night, she said: 'It would seem that I have acted precipitately, sir, and I must offer you my apologies. Would you believe that I was anticipating taking over the ranch myself?'

'Nope,' said Dick flatly. 'I guess I wouldn't believe it. I'd believe you were hoping to steal it, by force. By the way, four of your hired guns are dead. They went for their guns first. Two more, way back, are doing a little chore for me, mending a fence they were cutting down. How about these three—are you aiming to have them make any point for you?'

'No, they are under orders not to use any force.' She was so cool Dick couldn't believe it. It was almost as if she was forgiving *him* for something *he'd* done. Then she said: 'I think perhaps you and I should talk, sir, alone. We could go back to the house.'

He grinned at her. 'There's nothing to talk over, ma'am. You're on my land, and you ain't no way welcome. Just get riding, and take your gunslingers with you. I'll be along to the big ranch later to find out if O'Reilly knows about this.'

Angry spots appeared on her high cheekbones and her eyes were for a split-second murderous. Then the moment passed and she was cool and dignified once more.

'If I grant you are within your rights, sir, and
138

promise not to take up the shooting of my men with the sheriff—'

Dick lost patience suddenly. His eyes hardened and his jaw set around the cigar.

'Ma'am, I don't give a bugger who you consult about those four hardcases. And I'm a man of limited patience. Now get the hell off my property before *I* start using some force.'

His words would have set most women back, but not this cool lady. She actually smiled at him.

'You're a hard man, sir. You're lightning fast with your pistol. I like a man of your calibre. I assure you, you might find it worth your time, talking to me.'

Dick considered. Maybe he would learn something new. He still surveyed her with a bleak, mean face, when he said:

'Okay, ma'am, I'll give you ten minutes, is all. But we do it my way. I've no hankering to get back-shot. First you'll order your three men to drop their rifles and gunbelts to the ground.'

'And leave us at your mercy?' she countered. 'I don't think I could agree to those conditions—'

Dick's pistol appeared like lightning in his fist, hammer cocked. 'Then I'll order 'em to do it, ma'am,' he said. 'Besides, they've a chore to do before you leave, any of you. They're going to tear down that high fence around my lake. I've got good horses coming soon.' Jim now also had his gun out and cocked and aimed at the three men.

'Okay, you bastards,' snapped Dick. 'Out of your saddles and move it.' They obeyed, sulkily, evil-faced, and slowly. 'Now unbuckle your gunbelts and step over here away from your horses.'

The order was obeyed. Dick glanced briefly at Jim. 'Get their guns, I'll take their horses on up to the house. Hold a rifle on 'em, Jim, and see they get to work fast. I want to see that fence down by the time their boss-lady here and me is through jawing.'

Cursing and muttering, the three men went to work. Dick set off towards the house, leading the three horses back by the reins. The woman followed, dismounting and trying to keep pace with his long strides.

Dick tied the horses to a hitch-rail outside and went into the house. He was surprised at the interior. It was comfortably furnished and looked homely.

He waved the woman to a seat but she remained standing. 'Okay,' he said, giving away nothing. 'Say your piece ma'am.'

Little of what she said afforded him any surprise but he let her talk, just on the off-chance she might let drop some information he didn't already have.

'Tell me,' she said, cool as ever. 'Do you believe in justice? I mean as opposed to law?'

140

'It depends.'

'I'll take that to mean you do, given the right circumstances. Well, I believe I have the right reasons, and the *right* ... to exact justice of a murderer who has escaped for too long.'

Dick moved to place himself with his back to a wall and so that he could see through a side window, what was going on outside. He had no wish to be caught napping in the unlikely event of the men outside turning the tables on Jim.

She went on: 'At the time Beth married Grayson, Beth and I were close friends, had been for years. We exchanged letters. I do know that O'Reilly and Grayson were rivals for Beth. I don't think O'Reilly ever forgave Grayson when Beth chose him. Shamus did marry, but it was never more than a sham for him. I met my husband, my first, and married and we went to live in Canada. I suppose I forgot things Beth had written to me in letters before that—how she was afraid for Grayson, afraid somebody was out to kill him. Nothing happened at once and then I dismissed her fears and was wrapped up in my own life for years. My husband was a captain in the Union Army. He left the army when we married.'

'Your first husband's name?' prompted Dick.

'Collingwood. When he died I went back to Kansas. It was then, going through some old letters, I found those Beth had written years ago—'

'So,' said Dick. 'You made it your business to find out how things were with Grayson and O'Reilly, and Beth. You sent somebody to find out. Let me guess . . . could it have been a feller called Judd?'

She seemed surprised but it didn't shake her. 'Yes, it was Judd. And when I learned how Grayson was killed falling from his horse, and shortly afterwards Shamus lost his first wife, and then married Beth, everything seemed to add up.'

'And you took it upon yourself to cultivate Shamus, make like you were a friend, even married him . . . all to wreak just vengeance upon the man you alone had tried, judged and sentenced?'

'All right. Maybe it does sound . . . far-fetched. But since I married Shamus I've had all the proof I needed. Shamus has nightmares, and he talks in his sleep . . .'

Dick gave her a hard look. 'Again, ma'am, there is only your word for that—but, whatever, it is murder to take the law into your own hands. And if you want to know what I think, ma'am, that is one hell of a cock-and-bull story. I can't see you marrying him to gain revenge for your friend the late Beth—'

'Then you don't know much about women. I'll confess at first all I set out to do was to ruin Shamus, bring him right down into the dust, but then I saw a chance for myself to profit. As

142

his legal wife, I would inherit everything. But I didn't want to be saddled by a big ranch.'

'So you hired outlaws to run off his stock, kept the money, apart from what you paid the rustlers, and at the same time persuaded Shamus to quit, knowing he already had a lot of dinero stashed away? And that, ma'am, makes you a worse crook than you claim he is.'

'You're a hard man,' she said. 'You know how hard this country is. But it can be made easier, if you have money ... and plenty of it. Especially is it hard for a woman.'

'You needed help. Let me guess ... you persuaded Clayton to side you, and promised him, as his cut ... this ranch?'

'You are a very discerning man. Yes. All that is true. There were others, Barrow the sheriff, even the foreman, Anders. Every man has his price.'

'Which makes you think you can buy me?'

'I think so. But I know the price would have to be high for a man like you. It can be ... if you will help me.'

'What you mean, ma'am,' countered Dick sardonically, 'is if I'd stop hindering you. I think you're plumb scared since I bought into this. You're afraid I could blow the whole thing for you—'

'All right, if you want to put it that way ... yes. What do you say? I can see no profit for you in fighting me. Helping me, you could reap more money than you've ever dreamed about—'

Dick shot her a quick look and saw that she had said too much, and realised it too late. But he didn't press it.

'Okay, ma'am,' he said. 'I've heard you out. Was it you planned that fake bank robbery?'

'I planned it, yes. Every way I could make Shamus lose money I did it.'

Dick grinned but his eyes and face were relentless and bleak. 'That was your first mistake, ma'am. You see, your bank robbers stole my two horses—which dealt me into this thing. Your second mistake was thinking you could buy me off. Now I'll tell you again . . . get off my land.'

This time, stifling her obvious anger and frustration with great difficulty, she left, mounting and riding away stiff-backed. Dick told her:

'I'll send back your gunnies when I'm through. They'll be walking, so don't expect 'em back too soon.'

Three hours later, with the sun well on its way down in the West and long late shadows heralding a dark night, Dick, Lobo and Jim sent the three hardcases on their way. Half-an-hour after, they loaded the corpses onto the horses they'd kept back and sent these on their way back to the big ranch, with their grim burdens.

The seven cowboys arrived to start work around ten. Dick gave his orders. Their first job

144

come dawn was to bring in Jim's two thousand horses from the box canyon. Jim would accompany them. Then the seven were to remain armed to the teeth and patrol fences and guard the home ranch against a possible attack.

They slept, taking turns to stand watch, two at a time, all through the night.

At dawn Jim rode out with the seven hands and by noon that day they had returned with the fine-looking band of horses. The four gunslingers had been killed.

Dick had looked around the small spread, liking very much what he saw. A man could be happy, he figured, owning and running such a ranch, even after the range beyond was split up. Especially if a feller had himself a fine woman to give him kids . . .

He stood, several times, by the lake side, wondering. What the devil could be so all-fired important about that water? He was half-certain now that the answer was there, if only he could see it . . . the something else he'd been looking for all along, to make all the skulduggery worthwhile.

He dismissed the notion of revenge. Stealing the ranch, or the cash it would bring, maybe . . . but then, every time he thought about Clayton and his part in it, there came doubts. He had assessed the man himself as his own man and nobody's stooge. Shamus had declared Clayton was straight as a die, and a smart operator.

It made no sense that he'd be playing second-fiddle to a woman, even one as cold-blooded and ruthless as Mary O'Reilly. Maybe ... he figured ... just maybe, Clayton was smart enough to *pretend* to go along with the woman, and make his own plans to double-cross her in the end, taking the pot for himself? Dick had no doubts that it had been Clayton who had, ostensibly for Shamus, hired Sheriff Barrow. Anders had also had a part in that. Maybe the two of them were plotting something?

In the end he gave up trying to work out the ultimate answer. Yet he felt uneasy. There was, for sure, something nagging away there at the back of his mind, something he just couldn't put a name to. He ate lunch with Lobo and Abe and the men, one of the cowboys volunteering to do the simple cooking. They had finished eating when a rider came from town, at a gallop. It was Tim Grayson.

CHAPTER FOURTEEN

Tim almost fell from the horse as it slithered to a stop. But Jim Harper was already outside, there to catch him. Tim was pale as death, and plainly in agony. His wounds had reopened and blood stained his shirt and Levi's.

They got him into the house and onto a bed.

146

He blurted out his message before sinking back, his face twisted with the agony that wracked his body.

'Hell to pay . . . in town. A dozen hardcases . . . hit town . . . Clayton leading 'em. They released Barrow and the other two . . . killed Pollard. He . . . and the girls . . . got me under the bed before men came in. They . . . they grabbed the girls . . . saw 'em riding out . . . four of 'em . . . and they . . . took Emmy.'

'What about Abe . . . and the others who were loyal?' said Dick.

'In jail . . . Abe . . . Christ I'm in pain . . . and Olafson, Jakes, Penlow, Olafson's young son, four saloon heavies . . . Penlow and Jakes's men, and Carter and Cagney . . . they're planning on stringing 'em up at dawn just to show the town who's boss . . .'

He collapsed in pain. Jim Harper tended to him, bathed his wounds afresh, applied salve Dick produced from his saddle-roll and tore sheets to apply fresh tight bandages. Lobo brewed fresh Java and gave Tim a mug and stuck a lighted quirly in his mouth.

'Thanks,' grinned Tim. 'Jeeze . . . I thought I'd never make it. What are you going to do, Dick?'

'Rest easy,' said Dick, checking his side-gun and his rifle and ammunition. 'They'll never know what hit 'em, the bastards.' Leaving Tim to sleep, Dick placed a cowboy to guard the door of the bedroom, another with a rifle outside the house. He conferred with Lobo and Jim.

'We'll have to leave one hand in charge here— and hope to God we can trust 'em. The three of us have work to do in Lariat. Are you game?'

'Watch my smoke,' said Lobo.

'I'm ready,' said Jim, grimly. 'Let's go get the bastards.'

They split up close to town and went in slowly, separately, meeting inside the livery. Dick arrived first to be greeted, as he dismounted, by a big, ugly-looking man with bad and broken teeth. The man just had time to say: 'What the hell—'

Dick struck like a rattler, hitting the man flush on the chin. The other two joined him. They tied and gagged the man as he came round. Lobo stuck him in an empty stall, out of sight.

'One down, eleven to go,' said Dick, flint-eyed. 'Now let's see how many they've got guarding the jail...'

'You don't count so good for a heddicated feller,' grumbled Lobo. 'Counting Barrow and them other two, I figure there's still fourteen of the jaspers to account for—'

Dick grinned. 'You're dead right, oldtimer. I never was much at arithmetic ... Come on let's go. We'll split up, and keep your eyes peeled. Try to make it to the rear of the jailhouse. We'll meet again there.'

Ten minutes passed before they made it to the back of the law office building.

'Stay put, but be ready to come running and blasting with your rifles. I'm going to take a pasear down the side where the cells are.' Dick slid his gun out of the holster, arcing the barrel up and away from his body, thumbing back the trigger-hammer.

A quick check showed the alley between the jailhouse and the next building to be empty. But he knew they had to be careful. There were people about on the street and to start a gunbattle would for sure mean somebody innocent might die. He didn't want that to happen. He reached the cell windows and on his toes could just manage to peer inside. The first cell contained Abe, Olafson and his son, and Carter.

He tapped gently between the bars on the glass. Abe's face showed. The big man grinned. Moving back, Dick tried to ask what he wished to know, using signs and mouthing words. Abe seemed to catch on, and he showed three fingers, then made a rough star in the air, with one finger. Dick nodded and slipped back to the rear.

He told them what had happened, and said: 'There's only three in there. I think Abe was trying to tell me they were Barrow, likely wearing the badge again and his two cronies. We can take 'em ... but it's got to be done slickly and without too much noise ... no guns. Shots will bring the others around our necks and we don't want that until we're good and ready for 'em. And I want at least one of the bastards alive.'

'How are you figuring on playing this?' asked Jim.

'Lobo goes in boldly the front way. The back-door should be open, but we'll make sure first ... you'n me go in that way and try to take 'em from behind while Lobo keeps their attention.'

The small back-door proved to be open. Dick and Jim slipped inside and crept along the narrow space between a wall and the cells. The prisoners saw them but remained quiet.

At the dividing door from the cell block to the main office they waited, listening for Lobo's entrance by the front doors. They didn't have long to wait.

They heard the familiar raucous, bragging voice of Barrow exclaim: 'Well lookee here fellers, what just walked in, straight into our arms ... I always thought the old man was a sucker ...'

Dick eased the door open gently. He saw Barrow on his feet facing Lobo, and the other two a pace behind him. All three had their backs to the cell door. Lithely Dick stepped inside and Jim was a second after him. They moved in and brought their pistol-barrels crashing down on the heads of the two deputies. The men slumped to the floor unconscious. Barrow spun around going for his gun. He went rigid when Lobo slammed the muzzle of his rifle into his back.

They disarmed him quickly. Jim moved to the front window, rifle cocked and ready, and watched the street. Lobo found the cell-keys and released the prisoners. As they came out, each man helped himself to a rifle from the wall-rack and ammunition. They checked their loads and cocked the long-guns ready to fire.

The two unconscious men were locked in a cell, Barrow in another. Dick went in with him. He slammed Barrow up against the wall. 'Where have they taken the girls?' he demanded. 'Start talking, Barrow, or you won't live to hang.'

Barrow blustered at first but his true character showed after Dick had rocked his head back again with a sharp blow.

He talked. 'Four of 'em took the women to the Bar G . . .' he blurted.

Dick locked him up and surveyed his army. He grinned.

'Okay men, let's go take over this town again. Keep your eyes open as we go down the street, half one side, half the other. I don't want anybody innocent hurt. But shoot to kill when you seen Clayton or any of his hardcases. They shouldn't be hard to recognise. Let's go.'

As they moved down the main street, frightened women moved off the main thoroughfare with their children and men ran

151

for cover also. It was then Dick remembered that Lobo had got his arithmetic wrong also ... there had been a dozen gunslingers, plus Clayton, Barrow and the latter's deputies. One they had eliminated at the livery, Barrow and the other two at the jail, and four had ridden out with the women. That made only eight left. He turned to inform Lobo close behind him. The oldster grunted. Then, suddenly, he shoved Dick and threw himself flat.

Dick went down on one knee, turning as he did so. He saw the flash of a shot from high up and fired instinctively. A man's body came hurtling into the street from a roof across the street. Dick climbed to his feet.

'Thanks,' he said, as Lobo, back on his feet, joined him again. Both let their eyes range along the rooftops ahead. Those on the other side, now doubly cautious, were watching the tops of the buildings the other side of the street.

Then men came spilling out of the first saloon, seven of them, guns blazing.

Too late, Dick realised that one man having spotted them—likely he'd been in an upper room with a woman and climbed out with his gun onto the balcony, and from there to the roof—the shots had alerted the others.

He moved out, fanning his hammer and saw men crumple before him, to lie dead in the dust. Bullets whammed into the walls behind him, tore at his Levi's and shirt, and he knew Lobo was blasting away with his rifle close by.

While it lasted it was a hell of hot lead and gunpowder smoke. Then as suddenly as it had begun a deathly silence fell upon the street.

Cautiously, he and Lobo moved ahead, down the middle of the street. Others moved out to join them. The undertaker, the best time-keeper in town, was there almost before them.

Eight men lay dead, two wounded. The odd man to die was one of saloon owner Penlow's men, the two wounded were Carter and the Swede's son.

Dick left the undertaker to see to the burials. The two wounded were moved to beds in the hotel despite the protests of the fat owner, where they were tended to. The gunslinger from the livery was transferred to the jail and locked in a cell.

Dick was fuming. There was no sign of Clayton, anywhere in town. A thorough search began and ended when somebody informed Lobo that he'd seen the banker riding hell for split out of town when the shooting started.

'He'll have been making for the Bar G,' said Dick. 'And that's where I'm heading. But first, Lobo, will you stay behind and help Abe organise things here? Get men up on the rooftops again ... just in case there's another raid. Jim ... will you come with me? We've got to try to find the women and rescue them. I only hope to God they've not been harmed.'

153

They rode side by side in grim silence. Night was drawing in again and the wind was near gale-force, tearing at their clothing, their hats held on by the storm bands around their throats. The ride seemed interminable to Dick. Grimly they battled against the strong wind, their broncs giving everything they'd got, as if they sensed, through the hands and knees of their riders, the awful urgency.

The moon sailing high above them shone palely in the twilight sky, but later, the riders knew, it would be light as day, when full darkness fell. Short of the ranch house they stopped and approached with great caution, looking out for possible outlying guards posted. They encountered none. At the main home corral, they dismounted and tied their horses.

'Let's split up. I'll circle the house to the left, you take the right hand, okay? And watch out for the bunkhouse ... there's lights on there and we don't know how many men they have here. What we do know is that they'll all be top guns ... not cowboys.'

Dick was able to circle to the rear of the big house with its unrailed verandah right across the front, without a sight of life, human or otherwise. There were lights in the main room at the front of the house and now he saw a light coming from a second floor room. From the shadow of a large woodpile he watched the window. He saw Mary O'Reilly appear momentarily, then the unmistakable homely figure of Emmy.

Satisfied that the women were being held prisoners in the lighted upper room, he considered what next to do, how to tackle the seemingly impossible task of getting up to the room, and getting the women out.

He hunched behind the woodpile waiting and trying to figure out a way. Then he saw Jim, his lanky frame limned in moonlight as he rounded the far corner of the house. Showing himself briefly he called softly to Jim who joined him. They discussed the situation, thankful that for the time being at least, the women were safe.

'I don't reckon we have a chance in hell,' opinioned Jim gloomily. 'Even if we ... or one of us, made it to that room above, before we could get the women down the alarm would go up and we'd all be sitting ducks. Besides, we would need horses, ready saddled ...'

'Yeah,' said Dick. 'But let's give it a try, huh? You got an eye for a good bronc, and they'll stay quiet for you. Go pick out three good 'uns and if you can find bridles and saddles on the corral fence, get 'em ready. Have these and my horses ready ... right here behind the house.'

'What will you be doing while I'm risking my dang fool neck doing all that?'

Dick grinned, though he felt taut and tense, and anything but jovial. 'I'm going to get in ... via that upstairs window. There's a low roof just

155

below it. I think I can make it to that. If I can see inside from there ... sooner or later the women will have to be left on their own ...'

'Okay, it's worth a try. And I wouldn't swap jobs ... luck go with you pardner.'

Dick waited until Jim had been gone fifteen minutes before making his own move. Then, crouching low and keeping to what cover there was, he reached the side of the low out-jutting part of the house. He hoisted himself up onto this, frantically conscious that he was bathed in bright moonlight.

He crouched below the sill of the window, keening his ears, trying to catch any noise of talking inside the room. He couldn't hear a sound and decided he'd have to take a chance and raised himself to take a look.

He saw Emmy, Rebecca and Tess sitting on a bunk against one wall. There was no sign of anyone else being in the room. Cautiously he raised himself and tapped on the window.

The next second he cursed himself.

Mary O'Reilly moved from out of sight, to face him on the other side of the glass. She held a large Colt's .45 in her hands and it was pointed straight at his chest.

She held the gun in one hand, unlatched the window and slid the bottom half up.

'How nice of you to call, Mister Rufus. I rather expected you might. Step inside ... but first unfasten your gunbelt and drop it, and your pistol, inside the room,' she invited.

CHAPTER FIFTEEN

Dick unbuckled his gunbelt and dropped it inside the room. He stooped and swung a leg over the sill and climbed inside. At the instant he had both feet on the floor inside the room, all three women went into fast, silent action.

Emmy, big strong woman that she was, came up behind Mary O'Reilly whose attention was entirely upon Dick. Emmy wrapped a powerful forearm around the woman's neck, half-choking her instantly. Rebecca and Tess moved in, each grabbing an arm, pulling down and as they held her helpless even to cry out, Dick caught the gun as it slipped from her grasp.

Overpowered, Mary O'Reilly was quickly gagged and bound hand and foot with sheets from the bunk, torn into strips, and tossed unceremoniously onto the bunk. Emmy locked the door and slipped the key into her pocket.

Dick grinned at the three of them. 'I don't reckon you three needed me. Come on. Think you can make it out of the window? There's a low roof outside and I'll go first to help you off the roof. Jim's out there rounding up horses. How many hardcases are there in the bunkhouse? Did you have a chance to find out?'

'Yes,' said Tess. 'Twenty, and twelve more in town. She was telling us how she'd already taken over the town and next she was going to raid the Box G and wipe everybody there out.'

'Where does Shamus fit into all this?' asked Dick.

Emmy said grimly: 'He doesn't ... He tried to stop them locking us up. Anders shot him dead.'

'Okay, let's go ... and keep it quiet,' said Dick.

He buckled on his gunbelt, checked the load in the other gun and leaning out of the window saw Jim below, waiting with the horses. Changing his mind, he called softly to Jim and one by one helped out Emmy, Rebecca and Tess. Jim helped them down and they all quickly mounted.

'Okay, hit the breeze,' said Jim. 'I'll be with you in a couple of minutes.'

Dick led the way out of the home ranch yard, walking the horses, looking towards the bunkhouse for any sign of a man emerging from the front door.

Once clear of the ranch they urged their horses into a fast gallop. Behind them, using all his expertise with broncs, Jim opened the corral gates and drove the remuda out, some two dozen horses, slapped them into a fast run ahead of him, out onto the prairie. Dick waited with the women a mile from the ranch house. Jim caught up with them.

'I drove their horses off onto the range. Should give us a bit more time,' he said. 'It'll take 'em quite a time rounding up that lot again.'

'Good man,' said Dick. 'Now we ought to split up. Will you ride back to the Box G, Jim, get some sort of defence on the move? I'll take Emmy and the girls into town and see Abe and the others. There'll be an attack on the small ranch as soon as that woman gets her men organised and the town shouldn't be in any immediate danger. We're going to need all the guns we can muster at the spread. I'll bring some of them back with me. Will you round up all the ammo and guns you can find, and get the hands to put in posts and use that high barbed wire netting to run a ring of fence right round the house, about fifty yards or so from the walls?'

'You got it,' said Jim. 'Watch your back.'

He rode away at a fast gallop and Dick led the fast ride with the women, back to town.

When they reached Lariat, Dick wasted no time telling Abe of the development, and with barely time to drink a mug of hot Java, Dick was riding out again, heading for the Box G, and with him, in a tight bunch, rode Jakes and Penlow the saloon owners with their three men, Olafson, Cagney and Carter, making light of his wound.

Carter had dug out extra rifles and ammunition, and at Dick's request, a box of dynamite sticks with short fuses. Dick had insisted that Abe should stay in town and try to raise a small posse of men to defend the town, just in case the enemy made an unexpected switch of plan.

When they arrived at the Box G Dick was astounded to see how much of the defensive high netting had been already put up. The reinforcements quickly dismounted and lent a willing hand. Within an hour the horses were all safely inside a high fence which completely encircled the house.

Coffee and chow were prepared by volunteers and while they all sat around eating and drinking Java, and checking guns and ammunition, Dick talked about tactics for meeting the raid that he knew was sure to come, and soon, now.

'The main line of defence will be the house, a man at every window to cover all sides, two up on the roof—there's plenty of cover up there. When the raid starts one man must close the opening and wire it up to make the fence secure—this should at least delay any direct charge on the house. And when they try that first they'll have to cut a way through the fence. We should be able to pick 'em off . . . from the house. They'll have at least twenty men, all top guns and more used to fighting gun-battles than

160

most of you, but this one we have to win, okay?'

The plan received unanimous approval and Dick allocated men to their defensive positions.

Lobo, who had undertaken to do a scouting ride from town, at the request of Dick, arrived at the ranch soon after. He reported his findings to Dick and Jim.

'There's plenty bustle back at the Bar G. The woman must've raised the alarm soon after you got the women away. I saw her and Clayton and Anders and I counted twenty-four gunslingers. I reckon they'll be a while yet afore they can hit us here. Three broncs had been caught and when I come away, three of 'em were rounding up the rest of the remuda.'

'Good man,' congratulated Dick. 'Now how do you fancy volunteering for another risky job . . . along with Jim and me?'

Chawing at his tobacco plug, Lobo spat out juice and with a cackle, said: 'You name it, I'll do it. Can't let no younkers like you to out-do my generation.'

They joshed a bit about that then Dick was serious again. 'This will be Mary O'Reilly's last throw,' he warned, 'and she's going to make it hell for us here, while it lasts. I don't have to tell you that if she wins, it could mean the town's finished as well. It's not going to be a picnic, and some of us may die, but we've got to stop her, and Clayton and Anders. The house defence should be okay, but I think we need

161

something more ... just to maybe give us a slight edge. It has to be something the enemy won't be expecting. Now here is my plan ... crazy, yeah ... and the three of us will be outside the fence, sitting ducks.'

He outlined his plan and they went along with it, neither of them so much as commenting upon the danger it would put them in. They shared out the contents of the box of dynamite, checked that they each had a good supply of Lucifers and Lobo was hoisted to take up his position on top of the bunkhouse which was thirty yards from the house and afforded Lobo a good view of the house and yard on three sides.

Lobo settled himself with his rifle and ammunition and dynamite sticks, to wait for the attack to begin.

Jim's task was a little more risky and hazardous. He set himself in the high branches of a big tree on the opposite side of the house, carefully nursing his dynamite sticks in a small sack as he clambered into position, out of sight among the thick foliage. Once in position, he lodged the sack in a notch to his right and he, too, settled down to wait.

Taking the position with most risk attached to it himself, Dick took up his post in another tree, further away from the house, and beside the lake.

From this position he had a good, though distant, view of the main fence where he expected the raiders to stop, cut a way through and then come charging on up to the ranch house. Back towards the home ranch yard he also had a sight of three sides of the house. Time dragged by and waiting became a tedious and, for Dick, Lobo and Jim, an uncomfortable business.

Dick realised that this might be the real testing time. It would have been so easy to lose concentration. He gave himself up to thinking about the trouble looming and what had led up to this final confrontation. He had no illusions about the forthcoming battle. It would be ruthlessly fought and bloody. He'd been in a similar spot so many times before, and now he reflected gloomily on the greed and perversity of mankind, of man's inhumanity to man. Would there ever, he wondered, come a time when men and women were able to go about their lawful business without the constant fear of guns, or of those outside the law killing and robbing?

There were signs of a more civilised society starting to emerge from what the old pioneers had started, out of the mess of outlawry, war, murder and rape that had torn the whole nation for so many years. But the more he saw of men the less likely he thought the perfect kind of society men and women dreamed of, would ever become a fact. He was still puzzled about events that had embroiled him, once again, in intrigue and killing.

Considering what Tim Gordon had told him, against what he had learned from Shamus O'Reilly, and lastly the weird story Mary O'Reilly had spun him, the real reason for the trouble still baffled him. He was satisfied that Tim had come back only because Tess had begged him to do so, and to protect his own ranch. About the rancher, now dead at the treacherous hands of those closest to him, he still couldn't be sure. Had the stories of him killing first Grayson senior, and then his own first wife, been true? Jealousy in some people he knew to be a powerful and violent force and one certainly making some capable of murder. Yet, having talked to the rancher, he somehow couldn't fit the man with such a character.

Yet, Grayson and Shamus's first wife *had* died in odd circumstances, both falling from horses. And he couldn't forget that O'Reilly had claimed that somebody was trying to kill him . . . and had tried that same method.

Mary's story he found impossible to swallow. None of it added up to make sense, he figured. Why would a woman who suspected a man of having already killed one wife and a friend, go as far as to actually become that man's third wife?

Had she, maybe, been blackmailing the rancher? She could have been, and certainly Shamus wouldn't have told anybody about it. But away in the dark recesses at the back of his mind something kept nagging at him. He was sure there was something he'd missed, some tiny detail that could be the nucleus of the real solution to everything. He gave more thought to the woman. There was no denying that she was very handsome. She would have been attractive to most men. But there was also something vicious about her; a cold, hard, scheming ruthlessness that had come through to Dick instantly.

He could guess part of what had happened. Whatever the truth about the woman's intentions, she had clearly captivated and enlisted the help of dangerous men; Judd, Clayton, Anders ... and likely, at the beginning, Clayton's pardner, Joblin.

Had Joblin quit once he knew what was afoot? The story was that the man had been a mouse, scared of his own shadow. It could make logic. And if he'd run, for sure the woman would want him shut up before he could talk about what he knew. And Judd had been sent to kill Joblin. The interference of Fleetfoot, Dick's former scout, had forced Judd into killing Joblin in a way he'd not planned. There was no doubt Judd had been given orders to make Joblin's death look like no more than the result of a fight.

And all this had resulted in Dick's own involvement.

He had no doubts that Mary O'Reilly was probably the worst, most evil woman it had been his misfortune to encounter. He began to wonder about her first husband, sure that such a woman would only ever marry if she had another angle for so doing.

And suddenly it hit him. It came through like a flash of inspiration, the missing piece, the clue that had been lurking at the back of his mind for so long . . .

'Christ . . .' he exclaimed aloud. 'I guess I must be getting old. Of course . . . the feller she married was called Collingwood . . . Captain Collingwood of the U.S. Cavalry.'

He cast his mind back to a talk he'd had with a retiring Texas Ranger officer four years ago, Bill Johns. It had been Bill who had told him about the big gold robbery. A consignment of the stuff, worth millions of dollars, had been on its way north, escorted by troopers under the command of a Captain Collingwood. The convoy had been ambushed by four white men and a number of Apache bandits. All the troopers had been killed and, later, the Indians were also found shot dead. The gold had disappeared. Captain Collingwood, left for dead by the robbers, had recovered later, his wound proving to be only slight, though it had made him unconscious for a time . . . Dick felt excitement coursing through his veins. Then he started to apply logic. What the hell was he thinking about? That robbery had taken place twenty years ago, two years after the Civil War, in 1867 . . .

But the fact, his brain kept drumming at him . . . the fact was, the gold had never been recovered, it had never been traced. And the robbery, he recalled, had taken place somewhere along the trail between the Canadian River and the North Canadian River . . . which placed the spot near as dammit on the south Bar G range.

The sudden distant thunder of many hooves gave him no further time to pursue that line of thought. He now became instantly alert to the job in hand. The raiders were on their way.

He saw the party halt at the main fence, saw men dismount, pull on gloves and cut away a section of the fence large enough for the whole bunch of them to ride through.

And in minutes they passed him and were at the fence circling the ranch house.

A fusillade of rifle shots came from all sides of the ranch house and the raiders began to ride around the fence, circling it in the manner of Indians attacking a waggon-train. As they rode, the raiders fired at the defenders in the house. From his vantage point Dick saw two of the raiders pitch from their saddles. Then they broke off and dismounted slapping their broncs clear, taking up prone firing positions outside the circle of fence, some finding cover from which to shoot.

Dick saw rifle shots angling at the raiders

from Lobo and Jim, and he decided it was time he took a hand.

For a time the staccato shooting continued, bullets whinged into the house and struck the dust between, spurting up sprays like fountains of death. The air was thick with flying lead and then Dick saw two of the attackers run to the fence, crouched low, as the other raiders set up a terrific blast of covering fire.

Dick saw the cutters go into action on the fence and almost at the same instant the first dynamite sticks came flying through the air, the short fuses fizzing ominously.

The first fell short of the two men, the second right behind them, exploding as it hit the ground. There was an almighty explosion and nothing but smoke where the two men had been working on the fence. Dick lit a stick and hurled it, already lighting the second, and this he kept up, altering his aim slightly. More dynamite came from the tree where Jim was perched, and from Lobo on the roof of the bunkhouse.

The raiders started to make a run for it, only to be blown to pieces as they fled. For minutes the yard was a bowl of exploding hell and men were blown to smithereens. Then suddenly it was all over. When the smoke cleared, the scene was appalling. There was the awful stench of smoke and death, and not much left to bury. They found what was left of Clayton, only just identifiable. Mary O'Reilly, who had stayed on the edge of the fighting, died in Dick's arms, but not before she confirmed his suspicions, and late theory.

He rode with Jim, Lobo and Abe out to the Bar G ranch. Lifting equipment they found there further confirmed Dick's ultimate solution. He turned on Lobo and calmly said:

'You ornery, side-winding, hornswaggled, poker-faced, lying old son of a brothel madame.'

Lobo, mouth gaping, demanded: 'Why'd you call me all them things?'

Dick told him. 'You knew all along about that gold robbery twenty years ago. I figure for years you've been riding around these parts hoping to find where it had been hidden. If you'd told me, a lot of this hassle need never have happened.'

'I never meant to keep it ...' said Lobo meekly. Dick briefly told the others what he had discovered.

'The gold was stolen by four men, with Collingwood in on it. Each man took part of it—what they could carry. The rest was dumped in the lake on the Box G to be recovered later. Four of the men died in gunfights. That left Collingwood. He didn't tell his wife until two years ago about the gold. By that time he was dying of a sickness. And that was why Mary O'Reilly wanted the small ranch.'

During the next week all the clearing-up was done, and using the heavy equipment the woman had brought in, the missing gold was recovered and returned to the army. Dick was appointed to decide what was to be done with the huge reward.

At the end of the week Jim talked to Dick with Tim, Rebecca and Tess present. 'I've a mind to go sell up my little spread in Kansas and move here,' he said. 'If I could find me a nice little ranch.'

Tim laughed. 'Maybe you'n Dick can do a deal. I'm selling the Box G to him. He'll live there when he and Tess are married—'

Jim stared. 'Eh? Nobody around here tells me what's going on ... well, you Texan tornado ... how about you'n me becoming pardners in a horse ranch? What's Tess going to do with the big ranch?'

Dick said: 'Okay, it's a deal. Throw in your horses and we'll start even. The Bar G is going to be sold off in small holdings. The future has arrived at Lariat. Tim is going to marry Rebecca and ... well let him tell you.'

Tim obliged. 'I never had much hankering for ranching. I fancy myself as a newspaper man. Rebecca knows how to run the business. She'll soon teach me the ropes.'

Lobo, Abe and Emmy joined them. Lobo was looking miserable.

'What are you going to do with yourself, Lobo?' asked Tim, winking at Dick.

'Oh I dunno. 'Spect I'll just keep on riding around, git me another mule ...'

Tess laughed. 'No you won't, you old vagabond. It's time you settled down. There'll be a rocking chair for you on our verandah, and work if you want it. And you can be useful later. Our children will need a new grandpa...'

Lobo cackled into his chest. 'I won't say no to an invite like that. Mind ... I'm making no promises what sort o' grandpa I'll make.'

Abe reported that Barrow and the other prisoners had been taken by a Deputy U.S. Marshal for trial.

'And that about cleans it up,' said Dick. 'Now we can get on with the business of living...'

'And loving ...' said Rebecca, putting her arms around Tim.

Tess went to Dick. He kissed her. 'Aren't you going to propose to me?' she said. He grinned. 'Seems to me like that would be a mite superfluous. Go make us some fresh Java, woman. You might as well start learning—'

★　　★　　★

Later Tim and Dick, alone, talked.

'Do you figure O'Reilly did kill my Pa, and then his wife?' asked Tim.

'Yeah. I guess so,' said Dick.

Tom was silent for a time then he said: 'We must never let Tess know.'

'No,' agreed Dick. 'Let's forget it.'

171